CANDLELIGHT ATTIC

AND

ODD JOB'S

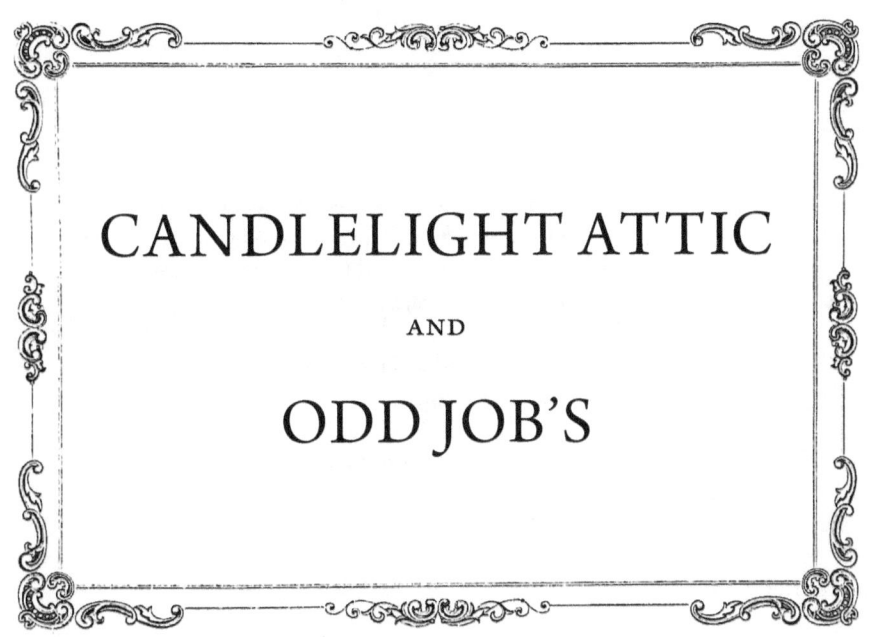

CANDLELIGHT ATTIC

AND

ODD JOB'S

By
CECILY HALLACK
Franciscan Tertiary
(Author of "The Happiness of Father Happé," etc.)

ST. AIDAN PRESS, LLC
Morning View, Kentucky

Candlelight Attic and Odd Job's.

Candlelight Attic: A Book containing Seven True Stories of the Supernatural, heard from those to whom they happened, and recounted with their permission in honour of the Seven Joys of our Blessed Lady. First published in 1925 by Burns Oates and Washbourne Limited, London.

Odd Job's: An Odd Book of Odd Stories. First published in 1930 by Burns Oates and Washbourne Limited, London.

Typesetting, layout and cover design copyright 2023 St. Aidan Press, LLC.

Cover art by Andrea England.

ISBN-13: 978-0-9719230-9-6
ISBN-10: 0-9719230-9-4

For more information, contact:

www.staidanpress.com
staidanpress@gmail.com

We have made no intentional change from the original text except to correct mistakes in spelling and punctuation.

CANDLELIGHT ATTIC

*A Book containing Seven True Stories of the
Supernatural, heard from those to whom
they happened, and recounted with
their permission in honour
of the Seven Joys of
our Blessed Lady*

To DEAR ALLA, from whom, frail and tender-hearted, I have extorted much and received more; and to my GRANDFATHER WILLIAM, patron of very early efforts, who at the age of ninety still runs upstairs, I dedicate these Attic Tales.

C. R. H.

Author's Preface

HERE ARE MANY collections of supernatural stories which sound as though they were true, and are written as though they were true, and even have a preface which talks about them as though they were true; yet the fact remains that the author has not said clearly and actually that he will vouch for them.

That seems to me a great waste, if they really are true. Parables are beautiful and often give their reader a glimpse of the author's vision, but they do not nourish and sustain the soul, as do what an old Protestant parson called "the pretty ways of Providence" by the very hearing of them.

I could tell many stories. They are the only thing I collect. But I decided to tell only those that were *first-hand*, and which I had heard from the lips of the people to whom they happened, if I had not actually been a witness of them. Most of them have been given me for telling as a thank-offering to God, and otherwise would never have been told. (But the sweetest will never be told, for they are keepsakes between souls and their Lord.)

This is a chilly world. According to the average person who "attends some place of worship," God is a most uncomfortable Person, tactless, avaricious and governess-y, never satisfied unless we are giving up something that makes us happy, or kneeling on aching knees. Such a One, it seems to me, ought to have instructed the birds to make their nests angular, lined with rubble. May we be forgiven the blasphemy of our peevish thoughts of Him. And we shall be forgiven, I think, because it is not so much that we are wilfully stupid, but that we insist in dwelling in dank disappointments and among fumes and frets, and not, as Juliana would say, "leaving the beholding of all tempests which let us of true enjoyment in Him." So we catch a permanent cold in the head and heart and are both miserable and stuffy and infectious.

Feed a cold. Here, then, is nourishment, and a fire that the Incarnate Word came to cast on earth and wills should be kindled. Come and get warm in this attic, this Upper Room. The candles are all blessed candles. And say with me to all who have generously given these stories: "God reward you," as the Franciscans do. And may it do your cold good. Pray for her who wrote them down.

LONDON,
Francistide, 1924.

CONTENTS

THE FIRST OF THE SEVEN TRUE STORIES

The Attainment of John Evangelist Wedgwood

or

The Sign of the Cross

CANDLELIGHT ATTIC

The Attainment of John Evangelist Wedgwood

or

The Sign of the Cross

IT WAS UPON THIS WISE that this story, and the six that shall follow it, came to be written. We were in the Stranger's attic—that is, the attic the Philosopher had lent him when the Stranger's one desire was leisure in which to be really ill. And really ill he was, else why should we have been sitting by the fire at something like two o'clock in the morning, talking of anything and everything and fighting the hideous black depression that was likely to kill him?

Imagine a long low room, blue with smoke—the Stranger liked others to smoke when it was forbidden to him—with the Philosopher in the corner, thrumming his harp and puffing at his pipe, and Father Paul with one long leg over the side of his arm-chair, and Olivia—Mrs. Henry Dacre, M.P.—all sable cloak and iris-blue dress on the other side of the hearth. And the Stranger in the narrow fourpost bed, occupied in holding the ball of my knitting wool.

The Stranger began to tell a ghost story—a bloody business of Jacobean days, when even ghosts were more coarse-minded than is quite to the taste of this age. Olivia said so, and told her own story

3

of a ghost in Dresden, who only trailed a ragged shadow into her room. Father Paul laughed like a bull, and scoffed at ghosts who had time for pointless errands. His own story was a most suitable one about the ghost of a poacher's mother who came and fetched him to take her son the Last Sacraments.

"How do you know," said the Philosopher quietly, "that Olivia's ghost was *not* on an important errand? A story does not always finish in the first instalment; sometimes it is to be continued in our next—in the next world. You are a materialist, my dear Father."

"Fudge!" said the reverend gentleman. "Give me another fill of your tobacco, please. All ghosts want are the Sacraments and prayers . . . from this world."

"You are all wrong," said I. "At least, I mean you are all beginning at the wrong end. The real key to a ghost story is, I believe, God's permission of it. That is the point to try and find."

"That you must think God's thoughts after Him, instead of guessing at the ghost's thoughts?" the Philosopher added for me, with his habitual comprehension.

"Exactly. And I think that Father Paul's ghost stories are the most elementary ones, the simple stories of the dead who want the Sacraments or prayers for themselves or those they love. And the Stranger's story is only diabolic journalism, which does the devil's work by putting more fear into the world, and only does God's work because nothing can help doing God's work in the long run. But I like Olivia's ghost best. There must be many more spiritual 'ships that pass in the night' than there are human, and think how many human beings drift by you if you walk down Oxford Street. What if they do hail you with some sign, and pass on? There is a fraternity among pilgrim souls. Besides, sometimes, they come on delicate wordless errands of inspiration."

"Tell us your ghost story, then," the Stranger said.

"I have never seen a ghost in my life," I said, "and I have never heard music, and I have never smelt violets or incense, nor tasted any mysterious sweetness. And that reminds me, give me the Stranger's medicine, Olivia."

"Come," said the Philosopher, "defend your thesis. You have something in mind, my dear, or you wouldn't have talked so fervently. I think I will tell one first, and you shall cap it."

And when I had settled the Stranger among his pillows, and refilled his hot water bottles, he began:

"This story I always call to myself 'The Sign of the Cross,' or 'The Attainment of John Evangelist Wedgwood.'"

"What?" said the Stranger, on one elbow. "John what?"

"John Evangelist—John Evangelist Wedgwood."

"Lie down, Stranger," I said. "At once."

"Extraordinary name," he muttered, and lay down.

The Philosopher ran his fingers over his harp, shook out a cascade of music, and pushed it away from him, and then continued:

"This story was told to me word for word, by John Evangelist himself, and I gleaned some more from his aunt, and I believe I can make you visualise it. It is the story of a small boy, whose father brought him to live with his sister-in-law when his wife died. . . ."

The Stranger interrupted by rolling over on to one side, so that he could see the Philosopher. But he said nothing.

"The boy was small, finely made, with a beautifully shaped head and nut brown hair as fine as silk. His father was a lithe laughing fellow, like a Florentine, who belonged to a great French family on his mother's side and an even greater Roman family on his father's. He was off to study the ancient civilisation of the Arabs, having some wonderful *entrée* to Arabian life—he was the sort of man who was always welcome, and who would almost have been allowed to strike matches on the Black Stone at Mecca. So John Evangelist was left with his elder brother's widow who had married again—a man who was something in the British Museum. Honestly, I think the father believed Mrs. St. Jacques—call her that—was the most motherly of women, because she called John

Evangelist 'sonny,' and gave him special cake at tea-time. So he left the boy with her, kneeling down in front of his son in the privacy of his bedroom, and making the Sign of the Cross on his forehead, telling him that there was nothing that could not be conquered with that Sign, and that he expected his son to conquer everything that was unworthy of his name—which was not Wedgwood. And on the small hand he put a heavy little signet ring engraved with a crest and motto on lapis-lazuli—'*Hoc facio ut vincam.*' 'Whatever you do,' he said to John Evangelist, 'say to yourself: "*I do this that I may conquer.*" And let no one but God conquer you, and Him serve with your whole strength and devotion.' And John Evangelist said: 'Yes, sir.'

"Well, the father went away, and John Evangelist stayed with his yellow-haired, pink-complexioned aunt who entertained him the whole day long, and showed him off to her friends and encouraged him to kiss their hands and bow, as though he had been a lap-dog who could do tricks. He used to be sent out to play in Kensington Gardens with sturdy little heathens who knew nothing about anything he loved. And at night, his aunt liked to come and what she called 'hear him his prayers' which meant that she sat and watched him while he knelt before his father's crucifix and tried to forget her, and had to say his little Latin prayers aloud to please her. Mercifully, he did realise that she didn't understand them, and thought that Gounod was the author of the *Ave Maria*.

"The first thing that went wrong was John Evangelist's nervous system. He began to find that tears came gushing behind his eyelids if he was annoyed by anything, and he was annoyed by many things every day. At night, more than once he screamed himself awake, and found a pink kimono bending over him, and scenting the air with *ambre*, emotionally motherly, and wholly uncomprehending. Then began the food trouble. He found it hard to eat. And one day there was the tapioca, and that was the first climax. He refused to eat it—politely and distantly at first, then autocratically, finally with direct anger. I believe what he said was something like: 'My God, I am not a dustbin.' Anyway, the parlour-maid went and complained to Mrs. St. Jacques, who had just that morning been reading a book on how to bring up a child, and rather fancied herself as the quiet mother who is obeyed. She spoke to John Evangelist, offering him the choice between tapioca and his uncle's library. John Evangelist rose, and opened the door for her, and closing it after her, ran ahead and opened the library door for her also. His uncle was out. Mrs. St. Jacques, who found John Evangelist's perfect politeness more than she knew how to deal with, pretended she had only meant to confine him to his own society until he was repentant. With a few well chosen words of grief, she locked the door, and let him hear her give the key to the parlour-maid.

"John Evangelist turned away. He considered the handing of him over to the parlour-maid had been the action of one who preferred to placate the parlour-maid rather than to preserve the decent deference due to one of the *signori*. It was a lack of honour.

"For some time, he wandered about his uncle's rooms which led out of one another, brushing his hair with his uncle's brushes and washing his hands many times with the hard brown Windsor soap because he liked it, and also . . . perhaps . . . because to be *soigné* was a comfort to his dignity.

"Then he went back to the library, and forgot the next couple of hours among the books.

"A shadow fell across the page like a reminding hand. It was growing dark. Now in his own bed, John Evangelist liked the dark, and the stars that were sometimes written across it like notes of a titanic plainsong, tones above human range of hearing. But at best, the library was a room endured for its books. To begin with, there was the Buddha, smiling at his knees and at destiny—a gold clad, Asiatic figure, antagonistic to every fibre of John Evangelist's be-ing, and to his eyes which had been taught in black and white and scarlet and blue, but never in that unglinting gold and blood-cruel colour of lacquer. Also, the walls were armed with Afghan spears and curved swords and shields uglier than any weapon. The luke-warm, argumentative, baldheaded man who was his uncle, had impressed on this room the personality that cowardice and convention had suppressed in him, a Moslem unreasonableness, fatalism and cruelty, without the true Moslem worship of the goodness of God. His uncle argued incessantly, and had never been known to come to a conclusion about anything, though he never moved from many a prejudice. He considered it narrow-minded to come to a conclusion about any fundamental principle, and was always waiting for 'further information,' much as a Modernist is always waiting for 'fresh light.' Black and white, scarlet and blue, were medieval to Wickham St. Jacques: give him the dried-blood colour of lacquer—spread it all over his room—curtains of it—carpet of it—the unanswerable colour of fatalism. He liked his huge flat-golden Buddha, because Buddha told him 'what will be, will be.' He would never have tolerated so much as an Arundel print of the crucifixion because it spoke of a Decision, of 'yea' and 'nay.'"

The Philosopher paused to relight his pipe, and to throw the match into the fire.

"I consider," he continued, "that sin is honest beside that kind of a thing, and when I visited St. Jacques, and was shown into his library, I disliked it more than I disliked the Rouge et Noire and the mill that had no gate on the road to . . . you remember that, Jane?"

"Go on," I said. "That is another story."

The Philosopher pulled at his pipe once or twice, but only Father Paul told him to buck up, and having done so, wished he hadn't.

"John Evangelist sat at the top of the library steps, which were high ones, because his uncle's bookshelves mounted to the ceiling, and the room was lofty. John Evangelist told me that the railings outside seemed to be like the spears of an invading army, and they reinforced those on the wall as it grew dark, and nobody came, and John Evangelist realised that nobody *would* come until he rang the bell and agreed to say he was sorry. He knew that would necessitate a lie, because he had done no wrong, and he did not intend to eat tapioca on this occasion or on any other.

"Then, it came to his understanding quite suddenly that he was being frightened. I put it passively like that, because he could not conceive *who* could wish to frighten him. It was not, of course, his uncle, . . . nor the Buddha . . . nor his aunt . . . and he doubted his being of sufficient importance to occupy the devil's valuable time. He considered it for some while, and realised that the whole room was his enemy. It was surrounding him with that sleepy assurance of the Buddha's smile. (John Evangelist did not know who Buddha was, but he vaguely imagined him as the Prime Minister of China.) John Evangelist realised that something must be done about it, because he found his body was trembling and he knew that the enemy had already caused that.

"'*Hoc faco ut vinkyam*,' he said to himself (that was the version he always read of his motto. He never could remember which word had the additional 'i' in it), and began to climb down backwards from his perch into the mob of shadows.

"His idea was to collect a few books that would be his allies. He found an Italian Bible (and probably never knew that it would be a modern Protestant one, printed in America by Wesleyans), and the *Vita Nuova* and a huge *Inferno* and *Purgatorio* with terrifying pictures that were homely to his memory. He added a La Fontaine and a Shakespeare in a rosy-coloured calf, because it looked so friendly, and a German spelling book, with chubby little pictures, and more I cannot remember.

"With these, he retired to a huge armchair, and made his fortress there.

"But after some moments, in the growing gloom, he realised that he had been forced to take refuge in a fortress. That was not strength. He rubbed his cold paws together, and said his motto over to himself, as his father had taught him, and then sat on his fingers to warm them, and stared at the room.

"Suddenly the house opposite pulled down the blinds, and a shadow from somewhere was flung half across the room, like a slave falling prostrate under the feet of the Buddha in the alcove.

"Imagine this in a great empty room, with walls that threatened with dead weapons, surrounded by a silent house—as silent as a London house can be when everyone is out and the servants are lingering over their tea in the basement that is under another room, not under the room in which you are sitting.

"John Evangelist knew evil when he felt it. He knew his familiar beads were in the pocket of his jersey upstairs. In his overall pocket were only cigarette pictures. He knew now, mysteriously, that it was something to do with his uncle—with the man who gave him money to go to the Zoo, and let him come and ask for paper and pencils and books. He knew that his uncle liked this room. That was enough. He was alone. His father was thousands of miles away. This room was smiling at him, and thought it had conquered him because it had made his hands clammy.

"He got to his feet, with his eyes on the shadow that lay before Buddha. That was the stronghold that would have to be taken . . . 'ut vinkyam.'

"As he moved, his chair knocked against the wall, a sullen thud of leather against paper-covered brick, but it brought down something that struck the ground and quivered before his horror-stricken eyes. It was only one of the old spears of course, but it was a declaration of war. It might have killed him, he thought. I think that improbable."

The Philosopher paused a moment.

"And then that trembling baby of eight shut his eyes, made the Sign of the Cross, and walked into the dark corner."

Olivia made a little sound. Her Michael is eight.

Dispassionately the Philosopher went on:

"They remembered him at nine o'clock that night—his aunt and the parlour-maid, with their consciences making them suddenly rude to each other. That would be about four hours after it grew dark. The room was perfectly still, and the first thing they saw was the spear. Then they saw John Evangelist.

"He was lying on the ground under the statue of Buddha, asleep. And he was sleeping as a child sleeps under the eyes of his mother, moving his delicate little mouth as though he were telling Someone what he had been doing. There was no trace of tears or fear in his face.

"His aunt told me that he looked like a child in heaven. That is all."

But it was the Philosopher who broke the silence again.

"Perhaps you don't think that is a supernatural story at all?"

He had to take our silence for the answer.

"He died four years later," said the Philosopher. "But ask Jane to tell you the rest."

They looked at me.

"Oh, shut up," I said, and walked to the window. "The Philosopher has no right to do things like that."

"What and why?" asked Father Paul.

"He has no right to use his occultism . . ."

"Thought-reading, my dear Jane, is hardly occultism," said the Philosopher. "I own I know no more than that you knew John Evangelist."

"I didn't," said I. "That's just it. I never met him in my life. But . . . why did you call him 'Wedgwood'?"

"Because that was the colour of his overall in the portrait I was shown."

I stared for a moment, and then the Stranger told me brusquely to play the game and tell what I knew.

"Well," I said, "I don't care in the least whether you believe it or not, but five or six years ago I was walking up Holloway Road one evening, and feeling tired, I jumped on a bus, and someone followed me, a small boy. I tell you, I never see things, and I didn't see this child, but I knew him with some senses I had never used before. He was a boy about eight years old, in a wedgwood blue overall. He slipped his hand in my arm—I tell you I saw nothing, but it was a great deal more real than if I had—and smiled at me, and talked about buses and the roads as a little boy does. I asked his name, and he smiled up at me without saying anything, and I called him John Evangelist, though I had no means of deciding *why* I did so. At the bus terminal he didn't leave me, and we walked along together for some way. I can't remember anything he said or did, but I had a sense of great and intimate consolation. I was puzzled as to who he could be, because I felt he was a real little human boy—somehow. I felt he had come because—for some reason—he wanted to be with me. And then, just before I got home, I lost him. That's the only way I can describe it. He didn't go. But I lost his companionship. Well, there was a letter waiting for me, with news so bad in it that I thought God had failed me. But I knew then why John Evangelist had come: to teach me that God does not always explain either His consolations or His seeming failure to hear our prayers. That is five or six years ago, and I am only beginning to see the reason for that terrible seeming failure. And it is only today I have heard who John Evangelist was. But then, God was a long time before He explained the joyful and sorrowful mysteries to our Lady. That's all."

"Not quite all," said the Stranger from the bed. "Not quite all. The Philosopher may know, or he may not know, but that is not all."

"I did not know until I had begun my story," the Philosopher replied, "and then I could not very well stop. It was best to go on."

"Best to go on," said the Stranger. "Best to let me have it, and have Olivia's face as you told it, imagining it all happening to her boy, and . . . Best to share the secrets of the King, for so God reveals hidden things in His own hour. I have waited a long while for that story. You see, I am John Evangelist's father."

THE SECOND OF THE SEVEN TRUE STORIES

The Bright Companion

The Bright Companion

THE PHILOSOPHER's veranda looks over miles of Surrey country, common land where the gypsies light their fires in the evening, meadows heavy with buttercups, and woods of silver birch and oak. The Stranger's bed was drawn to the window, and the rest of us sat on cushions round the wide stone ledge, leaning against the parapet, watching the stars tremble through the fading sunset. Olivia had a fat baby, the last of her sons, lying across her knee, blowing bubbles to himself and winking sleepily as the light played on his mother's rings. Father Paul was drawing caricatures. Then there was Maris de Lisle, slim in her black dress, and more content in her sorrow than many a woman on her honeymoon. And, of course, there was Cambrilles, a plain brown and black dog, too large to be a pet and too small to be a watch-dog, mauled and maligned by the whole household, and still smiling. He sat on the Stranger's bed—rather more exactly, on the Stranger—and appeared delighted with the Stranger's opinion of him.

"Haggis hound, that's what you are. And you weigh a ton. Hideous barbarian! Your only pleasure is in being kicked and cuffed, and you have no culture whatever."

"I am not so sure," said Father Paul. "The day I turned the soda syphon on him, he went straight to where the Philosopher keeps the whisky and sat up and begged."

The baby blew a derisive bubble.

"Never mind," Maris said. "Never you mind, my little mongrel.

If Jane or I want to stroll round the common before we go to bed, we are very glad to have you sauntering ahead."

"Yes, bless you," I said. "And you are the only hot water bottle that doesn't need continual filling. The Stranger has you and goes to sleep, and when he wakes up you are just as warm as when he went to sleep."

"Jane's idleness should be a matter of prayer amongst us," said Father Paul. "There are no buttons on one of my tennis shirts."

"You'll get fat, Jane, and then you'll puff and blow when you run upstairs, and nobody will love you." The Philosopher pointed each word vehemently with his pipe stem, and then put it back in his mouth with an air of finality. But he took it out again to say: "Give her the baby, Olivia, and tell us a story. It is your turn."

Olivia is perfectly able to write a speech or plan a motor tour with one baby on her lap and another climbing round the back of her chair. But the Philosopher always gives away her children to various suitable or unsuitable people when he wants her to do anything. You will find the young gardener considerably hindered with Remi (aged two), or Father Paul saying his breviary with one eye on the book and the other on Michael. If their long-suffering father is to be had, the Philosopher takes the whole four of them away from Olivia as though they were cushions, and sets them all on Henry. I digress considerably. (But not without reason, because it will give you insight as to the methods of the Philosopher as a host.)

But Olivia refused to give up little Henry.

"I haven't any story," she said. "And little Henry ought to have been in bed ages ago, but he *is* so nice. There ought to be a story about Cambrilles."

"There is," said Father Paul. "I was going to Mass this morning, and Cambrilles met me in the hall when I was just remarking to myself that I would say a Mass of one of the martyrs. Bless me if that dog didn't run into the morning-room and bring out a table napkin and lay it at my feet."

"Well. . . ?" we all said.

"White vestments," said Father Paul. "I had promised Maris to say a Mass of the Holy Angels for her. He knew. Remarkable dog."

Even Cambrilles shook his head and looked grieved at that story.

"Why a Mass of the Holy Angels?" The Philosopher can ask questions without being curious.

Maris smiled.

"Now that *is* a story you would like," she said.

"At last," said the Stranger. "Bang up my pillows, Jane. Gas, gas, gas, and twaddle, twaddle, twaddle, and when I ask for a story every night, you all say that is easy. And Mrs. de Lisle is the only one who comes to the point. Augh! Chilly! Dog, here! Put him under the cover, Jane. Now then."

Maris began, without preamble, in her soft Scottish voice.

"When I was first engaged to Lovat I was so happy that I began to think a good deal more about God. I began to go to Mass every morning because Lovat did, and we used to say that it didn't matter our being fifty miles apart, because we were both at Mass at half-past seven. So every morning I used to get up before seven and walk uphill for half a mile to church. After a few weeks, I began to get tired of my walk, and of sitting in the little tin church and feeling rather faint. And I began to argue to myself that I got over-tired. Now I think I certainly *felt* over-tired, but I never took the least harm, and a few hours later in the day was no more tired than if I had stayed in bed for another hour or so. However, I argued that to feel exhausted morning after morning could not be good for anyone, so I began to go less frequently, and there were plenty of mornings when my alarm clock did not wake me with its horrid noise. Well, one morning at about half-past six there came a voice into my sleep, a voice without sound, if you understand, but each word perfectly clear. '*Go and pray for those who cannot pray for themselves,*' it said. I was broad awake, every trace of sleep gone, and you may imagine that I did not lie in bed any longer that morning. It had been a perfectly quiet and unemotional voice, but ... I can only describe it as the voice of one who had newly come from watching over suffering, like a nurse who has had a sleepless night over a sick child.

"The days went on, and gradually I began to find the same exhaustion very trying. You understand, it didn't last much after breakfast, but in the rather stuffy little church, where I usually answered the Mass, sometimes two Masses, the feeling of faintness and the headache made it hard to pray anything but a prayer of what I am now at least wise enough to know is a prayer of simplicity, of absolute patience before God, with a will united to Him, though the mind be only distracted and the senses disinclined for anything but a cup of coffee. At last I began to get fussy over myself, and I decided that I really must go less frequently. But one morning when I had no intention of waking for Mass, the same quiet, patient voice rebuked me—not this time for lack of charity, but with a more poignant reason. It said: '*How long will you keep the Child-Servant waiting?*'

"Of course," Maris added, with a little flush on her cheeks and a shining in her eyes, "I had never thought of Him under that name, nor have I ever seen it used in any book to my knowledge."

"And you think it was your Angel speaking?" asked the Philosopher.

"I think so," Maris replied. "The voice, I think, was the same both times, and the impression it gave me was exactly that of an angel-guardian. It might have been one of the holy souls, or even my subconscious self, but personally I am quite sure who it was. I used to tell Lovat that I knew my angel by his voice, and that he was not tall, nor bright, except with a light like the scent of a flower, and that as he had never spoken to me before in actual words, I thought he was an angel who was very silent. I used to call him Tacitus."

"So you say a Mass in thanksgiving because he doesn't scold you any more?" Father Paul suggested. "I call that diplomatic."

"No," Maris said, smiling. "I have a Mass said in honour of him and of another angel I once came to know. That is the other half of my story.

"It was during the War. Lovat was posted in the north of Scotland, and the doctor sent me relentlessly to the south—to Sussex. I wasn't one of those wonderful women who worked like men while their husbands were serving in the army. Having Lovat taken away from me brought back all the humiliating weakness of neurasthenia, which four of five doctors called long and different names. So I was sent down to find a cottage in Sussex, and there I was to lie out in the sun and air all day long. I was really too ill to go hunting for rooms by myself, and Lovat wrote to me that he would have given anything to help me on the long journey from Edinburgh, especially because I was taking all my possessions and making my home in Sussex . . . till Lovat came home."

Lovat had never come home, and the Philosopher drew a long breath at his pipe, and Olivia and I glanced at each other with blurred eyes, marvelling at the serene voice of a woman who had nearly died of parting with her man when he was safely at a post in Scotland, and yet now, in childless widowhood, could speak of her dead dreams without a tremor of bitterness.

"But . . . you know how perfectly simple he always was about his Faith and unseen things . . . he said he would lend me his angel to find me all that I needed, and to protect and help me. As far as I remember, I drugged myself with a novel in the train, and thought of nothing, but when I arrived at the village I had chosen on hearsay, and found there was no hotel, and it was already late in the afternoon, you can imagine I felt as hopeless as I well could feel. There was nothing for it but to leave my luggage at the station, and set out to make some attempt to find lodgings. I had made up my mind that they must be overlooking the sea and that I must have a kind landlady, but more I didn't know.

"Then, as I set out down the long road to the sea, I realised there was someone with me. He was no more like my own angel than Olivia is like Jane, or the Philosopher is like little Henry. He was a perfectly different personality. I had the impression of a very tall person, very bright shining, with the swift, strong step of one who is used to the road. We had no conversation in words, but he was so strong and bright and full of courage that he inspired me. Although the first few cottages I went to gave me little hope of finding what I wanted, I could not feel disheartened. At last I saw exactly what I wanted. A little house with big windows, away from the rest of the village, beside a stream that ran with a lovely sound down to the sea. The woman who opened the door I liked at once. When I told her that I wanted two rooms indefinitely, she looked as though it was too good to be true. She said: 'I think God has sent you.' She had only her rooms to let as a means of livelihood, and it was winter then, and no one wants rooms in a remote village in the winter. She was so good to me. I shall keep her friendship all my life. She wasn't a Catholic, but she knew how to pray."

"And the bright companion?" asked the Stranger.

"He left me at the gate," Maris said. "Little Mrs. Brown was all the angel I needed after that."

She said no more, and none of us felt we could break the silence that had fallen behind the angel, because so soon it had become the silence of grief. Maris broke it for us.

"Had Lovat not told me he would lend me his own angel," she said, "I should have thought it was St. Raphael himself, because he is the guide of travellers, and I once knew a woman who saw him in the Berkshire woods, all in a glory of blue and purple wings, burnished in the heat of the day. But somehow I do think it was Lovat's angel, if you can imagine Lovat with anyone so splendid. I should have imagined his angel would have been the quietest, greyest angel in Heaven, and eloquent rather than splendid. But imagination is rarely right."

She was trying to lead things out of the shadow of Lovat's death, trying to make things easy for us, because we had known that rare, grey-eyed man who had loved her as few women are loved.

"For instance," she said, "one imagines Olivia with one of the cherubs—and I am certain he couldn't manage her when she is all cloth-of-gold, being rude to fat politicians at a political dinner party. And surely Cambrilles is angel to the Stranger, and yet that upsets theology, because Cambrilles is so full of such original sins."

The Philosopher looked at her with one of his queer piercing reverent looks.

"All I know about your angel, Maris," he said, "is that he is very content."

THE THIRD OF THE SEVEN TRUE STORIES

The Mind of God

The Mind of God

T WAS THE LAST HOUR of sunset—the first hour of candle-light, again. Already we were discussing the subject of stories.

"I've been thinking about these stories," Father Paul said, "and I do agree that the whole point of them is the insight they give to the Mind of God."

"Precisely," said the Philosopher, who was in a communicative mood. "The supernatural stories worth remembering and telling are those which make us realise God's attitude towards us and our doings. We are illogical students. We give months and years to the study of the mind of Shakespeare and Napoleon, but when do you hear it suggested that the Mind that made Shakespeare is likely to be even more interesting than the mind of Shakespeare? As for the stories of the powers of evil, at best, there's an awful sameness about them. They can only go the length of their chain."

"Personally," I interrupted, "I think we are badly needing to be told more stories that show what Juliana of Norwich calls 'the homeliness of God.' 'God is very homely,' she says, and I am always being made to realise that from experience. He is very courteous and very homely, and we are absurdly stiff and self-conscious with Him. I am continually hearing stories—exquisite ones—which would be proof enough to any soul that God is an Infinitely Understanding Person. But usually for the very reason of their nature, they are private—keepsakes between the soul and God."

"Especially in His thoughts for us when we are troubled about things we can't explain to anybody—intangible childish tragedies —things that are terribly real to us though they appear to be nothing," said the Philosopher, musing behind his pipe. "Appearances are only conventional illusions. There's an eye in the heart which can see the value of happenings."

"Well, there I'm an outsider," said my cousin Henry. "I leave all visions of the next world to the Philosopher."

"There you're wrong," I said. "If you don't reason out your charity on the principles of the supernatural, you are the most illogical idiot I ever met."

The others laughed. Henry's *protégés* are proverbially the most thankless, hopeless, easily offended lot in the world.

"Henry," said Father Paul, "is the rottenest philanthropist! What about Blinkett? He smelt like a walking pub."

"You can't blame a poor brute when his wife slings half the mangle at him . . . and . . . dash it . . . she pawned his boots . . . and . . ." Henry tried to explain.

"What about that woman whose rent you paid, and she complained to Father Paul that you didn't offer her a lift in your car?"

"Well, I might have done," said Henry.

"No," said the Philosopher, who had flagrantly stolen the third of Henry's sons, two-year old Remi, from the night nursery, because he liked an armful of baby while he sat in his armchair of an evening. "As a public benefactor you are quite a success. You provide Olivia with yellow amethysts and gowns like flag lilies and then let us look at her. You do not question anyone too closely when you find them in possession of one of your sons, as to where they got him from. You have political views of such an obsolete type that it refreshes me to explode them. But as a philanthropist . . . no. No, my dear Henry, in your charity you are a mystic."

"About my political views . . ." Henry began, but Olivia told him not to walk into traps quite so obvious as that one.

"Only a mystic would creep down the front stairs with a pair of trousers for a man at the door, hoping to avoid Olivia, and not know that Olivia was creeping up the kitchen stairs for a pair of boots, hoping to avoid you."

There was a shout of laughter from the bed. Henry and his wife delighted the Stranger, and these gatherings in his attic were the joy of his whole day.

"Only a mystic, "continued the Philosopher, "would collect the beggars you collect, people so poor that they've even pawned their self-respect to lie to you. A philanthropist only helps 'deserving cases,' as though any of us were that."

"Besides," said the Stranger, "a philanthropist always doubts gratitude. He expects it, but he doubts it. He thinks a man is only grateful if he thinks he is likely to need some more help from him. He doesn't remember that many of the poor are afraid he'll think them cringing if they are simple enough to voice the gratitude they feel. Philanthropy is the devil's charity. The charity of God . . . oh, the crucifix is the charity of God in one word—one Incarnate Word."

The Stranger had said that with such passion, that we were all silent and felt rather shy.

"I think the Franciscans are right when they say: 'God reward you!' for any kindness," I said. "Henry'll get the shock of his life, when he finds how Heaven remembers all the boots and coats he has stolen from his own wardrobe for beggars. Do you remember what Juliana of Norwich said: God 'wills that we wit the least thing shall not be forgotten . . .'?"

"I'll tell you a story about that," said the Philosopher, because Henry was beginning to rake his hair the wrong way with embarrassment. "A story about the things God remembers to fulfil and put right, and how things are linked in His plan. . . ." Cambrilles snored softly in the curve of the Stranger's arm, and Remi slept with his little wet mouth kissing his dreams against the

Philosopher's shoulder, and I sat with my hands idle in my lap. The candlelight was very soft, and the room very quiet.

"Come along then," said Henry.

The Philosopher began:

"I wouldn't tell you this story except for one reason," he said. "And that is because it is one of the stories that never get told. It throws a good deal of light on the Mind of God. I knew an old servant who said: 'His thoughts are not our thoughts,' when a child was run over or her pet cat died. But the truth is that His thoughts are not our thoughts because they are thoughts of absolute beauty which are often beyond the range of our understanding, as the ultra-violet ray is beyond our range of sight, and the scent of butterflies imperceptible to us. But, on the other hand, man is made in God's image, and man's mind therefore in the image of the Mind of God—so I am justified in considering that we are at least capable of *some* of the thoughts of God: of those that concern our little troubles and points of view. I own that there is a beauty we sometimes half-perceive that is so unutterably exquisite that it is more than we can bear. For instance, if you consider a lily or a kingfisher for more than a moment, you will feel rather afraid, and you will turn to something else rather quickly. My own opinion is that it is because we feel that, in a moment more, we should see the vision of the Thought behind the thing, behind the lily or the bird. And, not being contemplatives, we can't bear that piercing vision. But the vision of my story is human and won't pierce you. It happened many years ago. I was quite alone in the world. I seemed to be alone in a desert of the sands of time, knowing that year stretched beyond year, and I was alone in the silence. You would have thought this humbug if you could have seen me, because I always had company enough—the pick of the people who think and act. But I had no particular purpose in life, and there was the lack. All I could do was worship an abstract ideal of courage and think that somehow it pleased God, who was far away, reigning over eternity. I was quite a good Catholic, you know, but I was content to serve God as I served my country: I did not think of Him as the Mind with which man may commune, and in whose conversation there is no tediousness, and the beauty of whose Thoughts and Ways ought to be the eternal object of our worship.

"Well, it came to pass that I was in Stockholm, at a ball, why or how I forget. Everybody was an ambassador or a diplomat and the lightest conversation seemed to be important, and I was amused and bored with it. I was watching the dancing from a balcony that led out of a picture gallery which nobody seemed to patronise. It was pretty to watch such a beautiful, courteous, thoroughbred crowd, swimming through dance after dance. But I wasn't an ambassador of anything or anybody. So I looked on. Then I heard a door open behind me. I thought it was my host come to find me, so I kept quiet in the shadow of a curtain, because I didn't want to be found. But it was a girl with a little shining head of brown hair, who wore a dress of pearl-coloured satin, cut as severely as a nun's habit. I remember I noticed she wore hoops of pearls in her ears—a thing not then in fashion—and pearl buckles on her slippers, and no other jewellery, not even a star in her hair or a ring. She walked down the lonely room until she was opposite a mirror, and I thought it was her first ball, and she had come to admire herself, and I smiled and thought she must be very satisfied with what she saw. But she stared in the mirror for a minute, and then twisted her hands and drew her shoulders together as though protecting herself from something. Then she must have seen me in the mirror, because she gave a cry—a far more terrified cry than I should have thought a girl would give merely because she saw a man sitting and watching the dancing, when she thought she was alone. Of course I rose and came forward and made my apologies.

"She reminded me of a picture of the Annunciation. There was something in the way she held a great lace fan across her breast as though she did not want anyone to come near her. When I told her my name, I fancied she seemed the least bit reassured, but she did not take my arm when I suggested she should sit with me on the balcony and recover from her fright. It reminded me of a doe who would walk all through five miles of park with me, and who would take sweet cake from my hand, but would never let me touch her. The hunter instinct in me told me that this child—she was little more, it seemed to me—for some reason or other, did not want to be touched. So I did not sit beside her on the couch: I pulled a chair beside it, and she seemed relieved, and furled her fan and explained herself to me. She had not known I was there. The gallery had associations for her, and she had come there to remember . . . and she must have been rather strung-up. I answered her with some soothing commonplaces about the unwisdom of reviving any but the happiest emotions, and with a casual eye on the way the light flickered on the satin of her bodice as it rose and fell, I talked until she was breathing more quietly. I remember I said that it would never do for me to revive a hundredth part of the unpleasant emotions I had experienced, and I cheerfully told her a couple of the experiences that even now give me a nightmare or two—funny little experiences—no tiger ready to leap or of sleeping on a keg of dynamite and dropping a match, but experiences that have frightened the spirit rather than roused physical fear—a night I spent with a red-haired freckled little spiritualist on board ship, and an afternoon at Notting Hill Gate with an old man who founded two orphanages and was a damned soul if ever I saw one.

"'Remember,' I said, 'physical fear is a thing to be conquered, a healthy sort of a business; but fear in the soul is only caused by the devil, and is more poisonous than sin.'

"She looked at me as simply as though she were dying.

"'I don't know what you are,' she said, 'I know your name and that you are some kind of diplomat, but I wish you would tell me one thing: do you wear a medal of our Lady round your neck?'

"I fished it up. Had it since I was a baby, and I've given it what I thought was my last kiss many a time.

"'I'm not queer in my head,' she told me gravely, as though I shouldn't have known if she was in two seconds, 'but for a whole year I have been asking our Lady to send me someone who would help me out of my fears . . . and one who wore a medal of her round his neck. That was to be the sign I could recognise him by, beyond the fact that he would say what I needed to be told. Do you think our Lady sent you?'

"'Why, of course,' I said, easily enough. 'I think she did if I can be of any use to you.' I was answering on the broad idea that anything that helps anyone out of a fear is from Heaven. I didn't imagine myself to be an angel. I should have said the same thing of a dog, if it comforted her.

"'Oh, how good she is,' the child said, and lay back among the cushions.

"I didn't want her to imagine me with wings, so I began to make her laugh with a story or two, but suddenly she slipped up, and into the middle of the room where she had faced the mirror.

"'This is where I am afraid,' she said. 'This is where it happened.'

"I knew enough to realise that I had to do something—merely, on the plane of psychology, to break the train of association. So I pulled a great white lily out of the decorations and gave it to her.

"'Put that in its place,' I said.

"She looked as though I had brought the flower from Paradise, and for a moment stood there, dazed, with the lily to her lips. Then I coaxed her to sit down in her chair again, and she curled up, lily and all, looking more like a Fra Angelico virgin than ever. She was very silent. I must have chatted to her for another half hour, and then I told her she must come and have some supper. She rose obediently, but I didn't give her my arm. Somehow I knew I hadn't to. But as we crossed the room she hesitated and just at the place she was afraid of, she put her ungloved hand, not on my arm, but into my hand as a child does. I thanked her, and because in the ordinary way, one would have put her hand to one's lips—she was used to conventional ways—I kissed the flower she held instead, and she tightened her fingers with a sort of sigh of gratitude.

"I had better call her Drusille. That was one of her names. Her mother was the Duchesse de Something or other. At supper she laughed at everything I told her, and finding she had left the wisp she called her handkerchief in the gallery, allowed me to give her mine to wipe her eyes with. When I went to get her a third ice, my host accused me of baby-stealing, but I was a great deal happier than I should have been talking to the other people.

"After supper we went back to the gallery, and there we talked. What we talked about I won't tell you, but it concerned the forces of prayer and of peace. But at last she saw her mother looking for her in the ballroom below, and we rose to go. And then she told me.

"She was not such a child as she looked—old enough, at least, for a man to have made love to her three years ago in this gallery. On three separate occasions she had been alone with him there, and only on the third time had he revealed himself as he was in truth. A woman of the world would have forgotten it in a month, but Drusille was not the kind that forgets. And yet it had all been a mere nothing.

"'It was only that he touched me,' she said. 'The first time he only once touched my arm, as a brother might, but . . . And then the second time, he gave me a little yellow lily with a scent that laughed at me for being young, and the third time . . .'

"She was standing in the middle of the room again, with her finger-tips on my arm, and the lily in her other hand, and the shadow in her eyes. I was afraid more had happened than she would tell me, and I wanted to have the whole thing said and dealt with. But she looked up at me, and told me . . .

"'The third time he looked at my eyes and put his arm round me, and now he's dead and he keeps telling me that he holds me so.'

"You can smile at me when I tell you what I did, but I did it at the bidding of some invisible counsellor. I drew my sword, and I slashed round her, making the sign of the cross with the blade, and then I bade her show me where he had touched her arm. She showed me, and I scratched myself with my sword, and made a cross with the blood on the white skin. She didn't seem in the least afraid of it.

"'There now,' I said, 'that's my challenge. I may see more of the gentleman, but you never will.' And I bade her pull her sleeve over the place, because we could hear someone coming. It was her mother, who thanked me for amusing Drusille.

"'Has she told you that she is off to Carmel next week, and finds balls rather a bore?' she asked me. Then I understood a good deal.

"When her mother went out of the doorway the child managed to say good-bye in her own way. She put her lips to my sword. I never saw her again, nor even heard whether she is alive or dead. My business was finished."

"Was it?" the Stranger asked, in his sharp way.

The Philosopher smiled.

"Shall we say that the romantic part was finished?" he replied.

"The romance was like the colour of the kingfisher," said the Stranger. "But the colour is not all. Tell it to the end."

"Well," the Philosopher said, "the rest was what I had expected. There was someone who tried to throttle me in the night. There is a sort of a bruise like a dirty thumb mark on my neck somewhere. But at last I managed to say the Holy Name . . . and my assailant left me. He took with him the sense that I was aimless and far away from God. I knew I was not left out of the plan of reconstructing all that the enemies of God had laid waste. He had sent me to repair every detail of those three interviews in the very place where they had happened. And every time I shave I see that mark, I remember that I have at least served God's purpose once. He turns everything to His purpose, even the garlands of a ballroom—a dress-sword and a man who thought he was forgotten."

THE FOURTH OF THE SEVEN TRUE STORIES

He Held His Peace

He Held His Peace

OONLIGHT FLOODED the floor. The clock ticked. The wind, coming through the wide windows, stirred the bed curtains and valance. And the Stranger shifted among his pillows, tired out with sleeplessness. The air was so sweet and so cool, but he was oppressed with one of his moods. He would lie on one side, staring out over the meadows that lay shining in their heavy dew under the moon; then he would toss over to the other side and look at the low roof of the chapel and the red spark of the sanctuary lamp and mutter half a prayer; then he would fling himself on his back and talk to me. He had asked me to sit in the rocking-chair and knit, to stop knitting and read to him, to stop reading and to sing ballads, to stop singing and to talk to him, and then to stop talking and come and rearrange all his pillows for the twentieth time. But it was all in vain, sleep was not to be found anywhere. To tell the truth, I was not anxious that sleep should come, for it would not have rested him. It would only have been the heavy sleep of exhaustion into which he sometimes fell, only to twitch and groan and wake with a gasp of fear. His spirit was unquiet. What we were really seeking was peace, rather than sleep.

"Jane," he said, "this is an interminable night. Can't you do anything?"

"Shall I give you the rose pillow?" I suggested. It was a silk and muslin cushion of pot-pourri, made from the roses that had faded on the altar, and often this would soothe him curiously.

"No," he said, kicking the dog who enjoyed eventful nights on the foot of his bed, "none of your old wives' potions will do tonight. And I don't want to be stroked or dosed with a milk-and-water bromide. Get your book and read Compline again."

"But it is nearer time for Matins and Lauds," I said.

"Don't argue."

But before long he stopped me, speaking wearily with his gaunt face in shadow, and with a deeper shadow over his mind.

"That's all true," he said. "*Mine eyes have prevented the watches, and I was troubled and spake not. I have been thinking of the days of old, and I have had in my mind the eternal years.*' God is perfectly silent. I cry to Him, but He makes no reply. And that silence is heavier than I can bear. The world is all awry. It's ignorant and unhappy. There is no peace in the world. And yet God is silent. And think of the eternal years of His reign, and the days of old, what a fool I've been, and what fools almost everyone has been, and how we all have never given Him a thought for months at a time, and we go our own ways and make havoc of His world, and He never says a word. It's weighing on me, that silence. One can hear it, in the night when one's not far from death. It's too big for me. You'd better fetch the Philosopher."

I met the Philosopher on the stairs.

"Were you coming up?" I asked. "The Stranger wants you."

"Yes," he said, "I was coming up."

His swift, quiet footsteps down the landing were strangely good to hear. The softest whisper at his door will always be answered in a moment, but again and again he meets you on the stairs. It is as though he were conscious, even in his sleep, of anyone needing him. I have never seen him half-awake, or troubled by a summons.

The Stranger welcomed him with a gesture.

"How you'll enjoy good nights when I am dead!" he said. "I'll not lie awake for more of these nights than I can help. I am bored with existence. Come and read me Baudelaire."

"On a homœopathic principle?"

The Philosopher stood beside him, playing with the cord of his dressing-gown, apparently sleepy, but awake to every sign of the Stranger's mood. The Stranger smiled, and pushed the little silk-bound *livret* across the counterpane.

"On the principle that any kind of human utterance is better than the silence of God: and Baudelaire felt the silence very well."

The Philosopher threw the little book out of the window.

"Talk sense," he said. "You're not in the least feverish—you're below normal. You can go to bed if you like, Jane."

"No," the Stranger said, "she can't. I may want her. She can go to bed when I'm in my coffin."

"I'd better stay," I said. "You never could fill a hot water bottle."

My lamp, with its cowslip-coloured light, was the only illumination in the attic, but the Philosopher struck a match and lit a couple of candles underneath the crucifix that hung over the prie-dieu.

Then he pulled up an armchair, and settled down to be good company.

"Now," he said, "talk about your thoughts."

The Stranger was looking ruefully after his Baudelaire, whose exquisite hopelessness would be beyond deciphering when the dew had done with it.

"And so, farewell," he said, waving his thin hand towards the window. "What simple and effectual methods you have, my dear Philosopher. Well, I was saying that God is very ominously silent. Do you remember that crucifix that hangs outside an Anglican church near Charing Cross Road? You always see it. And it has written underneath: 'The Lord shall reign.' It is so ominous. He is silent. He is biding His time. And that bodes no good for sinners. That silence has the heaviness of hell in it."

"It bodes no good for the fiend," the Philosopher corrected. "His silence is the silence of one watching—watching over us who have claimed sanctuary of His peace."

"But He is not watching over sin."

"No. Then His silence is the silence that fell after He said: 'It is finished.' It is the silence of the Conqueror, for the conquest is accomplished in Eternity, no matter whether the battle is only begun in Time. God is silent because He has already said: 'I have overcome the world.' He said that before He had paid the debt—in Time: before He was crucified, because He said it at the Last Supper when Judas was just accomplishing his betrayal. He said more; He said: 'Now is the Son of man glorified' when a shameful death lay before Him, and even the apostles would forsake Him and flee."

The sick man was at the mercy of his moods tonight. His faith was overcast. He was enduring the slow exhausting of his physical life, with all the sensitiveness to heat and cold, the wandering neuralgia, the thirst and hunger and disgust of food—all the weary ailments of a worn-out body. His knowledge of the world burnt like tinder under his sarcasm and cynicism, and he realised his ignorance of eternal things. His faith had been a great and noble loyalty to the Faith of his fathers, but he had not studied that Faith, and now he clung like a child to all that he knew—the Mass, the Gospels, the crucifix, the beads that had been his mother's. Nothing eased him for long but to be told more about eternal and mystical things, and, lacking that, he would play with his poems of Baudelaire or one of the vain, elaborate agnostics of the moment, as though to show up their miserable folly beside the undeniable fact of death.

Now he signed to me to fill his hot water bottle afresh, feeling the dawn chill in the warm night air.

"Well, my dear Philosopher," he said, "I have been a respectable Catholic. I have gone to Mass and made my Easter, and I never had a taste for women or wine, and I never murdered anything except tigers, and I haven't talked scandal about other sinners, but this dying is a business I haven't practised. One's wits get sharpened— like one's bones. Jane, my left hip-joint is boring through the mattress. There is a force that comes to me and tries to depress me back and back into hopelessness and horror. It walks about in the darkness. It is the terror in the night of one's ignorance. It talks to me and threatens me, and I appeal to Him, hanging there on the crucifix, but He never says a word."

"No," the Philosopher said, "He never answers back to the fiend. He merely goes on reigning from the Cross. Would you like to hear the story of that crucifix?"

"I know. Jane painted it, the wounds and bruises. She told me when she was painting me with methylated spirits."

"She didn't tell you the story, because she doesn't know it. I had that crucifix before I was a Catholic."

"I never knew you had been anything else," the sick man said with some interest. "I can't imagine it—unless you were a very humble sceptic."

"I had that crucifix when I was merely a man who believed in God and the difference between good and evil, and in life after death. I had been in America, and I had met some of the people who were investigating occult subjects, in the wake of Madame Blavatsky. It was what finally came to be theosophy, but then it was merely occult investigation. There was plenty of trickery and cheating, but there were plenty of good and sincere people investigating as scientifically as they could. They claimed to get into touch with the dead, and the newspapers behaved as though no one had ever made such a statement before. I lectured on all such things—historical lectures, on divination, and the oracles, and black magic, and so on. But when my business was done, and I was back in England, I determined to make investigations for myself, so as to have first-hand information for my lectures. It was all rather small and silly after Indian occultism, but I set about it. I began with planchette, as most people do, and with success. I wrote for hours at a time, receiving some communications which convinced me, as I wanted to be convinced, that at all events the information did not come from my own subconscious mind. I was personally satisfied that I was in communication with a spirit or spirits other than myself. But although I was under no impression that I was talking to the angels or persons in heaven—for my controls claimed to speak from what we should call purgatory—I was not, at first, doubtful of their good intent.

"One night, alone in this room, and sitting a little nearer to the fireplace than I am sitting now, I asked my control whether it would be possible for him to give some visible manifestation. The answer in automatic writing was: Yes. I then asked how; and I was told to look steadily into the further corner of the room, past my prie-dieu, which was there just the same then, because I always professed faith in Christ. So I did as I was bidden, and after a moment, I saw clearly but not distinctly, a figure standing there in the corner. I was not satisfied, but I asked, by means of the planchette, that it should come nearer and show itself more distinctly. The answer came at once: it could not come nearer because of the crucifix which hung between us; I must take that down.

"Now you must remember that I was not a Catholic and the crucifix was only a plaster figure on a wooden cross, unblessed and bought in a shop. Keen to continue my experiment, I went to take it down. The moment I lifted it off the nail, I could hardly hold it. Someone, like a very strong man, seemed to be wrestling with me for it. I was in good condition—I used to run my three miles before breakfast—and I was a fairly good lightweight boxer, but I had to put forth all my strength to hold it.

"And then I realised that I was being asked to surrender the holiest symbol the world possesses, and I knew what to do. With all my might I held it, and turned and walked straight up to the apparition . . . right through it . . . and out of the room into my bedroom. There was no one in my study when I returned to enthrone Him again."

The Philosopher pulled out his pouch and began filling his pipe.

"What did you feel, when you walked through the thing?" I asked.

"As though I was at a cross-road with four winds blowing on me."

"And all the time He said nothing?" the Stranger asked.

"It led me seriously to learn of Him, and I began to study Christian mysticism more carefully, and before long I came home to the Faith, but no: He did not come down from His Cross or answer them a word."

Above the woods on the horizon I could see the first welcome colour of the dawn. The sick man saw it, and rested his head among his pillows, and I knew that his eyelids would yield suddenly to sleep, and that his spirit would not disturb him with its restlessness. He seemed to be listening to the silence as though he found it good.

But the Philosopher finished his own train of thought.

"His reply is the reply He makes to all His enemies and to ours—to all who think to prevent His ultimate victory—the reply He made to Pilate: He held His peace."

THE FIFTH OF THE SEVEN TRUE STORIES

Lumen de Lumine

Lumen de Lumine

CAME UPSTAIRS after dinner and found the attic sombre and still.

"Awake, Stranger?" I asked.

There was a movement from the bed, and the Stranger turned his face to me, away from the wall.

"You've been a long time at dinner," he said. "It has been like an old forgotten backwater up here. I am tired. I have come a long way away from all that . . . the talk and the pretty lights on the table. It seems a funny existence you have down there. Up here, one is just alone with the truth . . . one's own poor soul, and the aching bit of clay one calls a body, and the darkness, and one's Maker."

"You've evidently been with yourself," I said, attending to the fire. "Being with God doesn't make people dismal."

"Oh, I've not been exactly dismal," he said—"only rather rueful about the wreck of a lifetime."

"Never mind about your lifetime," I said. "That's all forgiven and forgotten. And you've a whole eternity to love God in, and nothing to prevent your beginning now. Death won't interrupt you. Let me turn your pillows and pull the clothes straight."

"Who's at dinner?" he asked. "I fancied I heard Henry correct somebody's politics three floors below."

"Captain Rushton, Olivia, Mrs. Derwent, Henry, and . . ."

"What's Olivia looking like?"

"Herself."

"She will come up?"

"Doesn't she always?"

"Still, go down and tell her I want her."

But I knew whose fingers were tapping on the door, and bade her come in. The fire was low, but I had lit a couple of candles, and the Stranger could see her clearly. She had a dress of soft ivory lace, her favourite yellow amethysts, and an ermine cloak.

"How is our patient?" she asked. "Did you have some of that soufflée, Stranger? Wasn't it good?"

In the candlelight she looked like the Belle Dame sans Merci. The Stranger rested his eyes on her.

"No," he said, "it was nasty. Like Sunlight Soap. Where are the others? Coming up?"

"Yes. Evidently we are *not* amused tonight."

"Not amused by hearing all the chatter far away downstairs, and being all in the dark up here. You look like the flame of an unearthly candle. I am so tired. I have seen no one but Jane all day since breakfast. And there has been no sun."

"Well, I meant to come over and see you after lunch, but Michael tried to shave Remi with a knife, and cut the child's face in so many places that both Nannie and I had to set to work to plaster them. And then I had a speech to write about Captain Rushton's scheme, and I brought him over here to dinner when I had finished asking him questions."

"And I have brought him upstairs," said the Philosopher, coming in. "Captain Rushton, the Stranger. Mrs. Derwent, the Stranger. Stranger, Captain Rushton has a story for you, and Mrs. Derwent has another. For your sake I s'hush-ed them and rushed them upstairs, before they could begin in the drawing-room."

Mrs. Derwent was an elderly woman in a plain grey gown, with magnificent diamonds which caught the candlelight and played with it. The light shone on the men's shirt-fronts, and when they had settled round the fire, the room seemed a great deal brighter. The Stranger, I knew, was hungry for light.

"You are very kind to a bedridden wretch," the Stranger said. "I cannot tell you how much I appreciate it. The days are long, especially when they are sunless, like today, and when one is sitting in darkness and the shadow of death. There never was a child more eager for stories than I am."

I liked Mrs. Derwent's kind face, and Captain Rushton's pleasant one.

"Well," Rushton said, "mine is not a story at all. It is an incident. But I believe Mrs. Derwent's is a beauty."

"Tell yours first," the Philosopher asked him. "It will do as a prelude."

"Very well," he agreed, settling back in his chair. "My story is this. I was staying in an old house in Worcestershire which dated back to the fourteenth century. It had once been part of some monastic buildings, and one of the rooms, now used for storing grain, had been the chapel. I had discovered that the old altar-stone, with its five crosses, had been built into the window as an inner lintel.

"One wet and stormy night I realised that I had left that window open, and the grain would be getting wet and turning mouldy. So I went to that room to shut it. You know how lonely an old house is on a dark and stormy evening—an evening rather like this? And especially the upper rooms that are not inhabited. Well, I went along the passage and opened the door. The window was open. But underneath was the old altar-stone. And the five consecration crosses were blazing with light."

That story interested the Philosopher. He stuffed the tobacco into his pipe very thoughtfully.

"Yes," he said, "and no one likely to come there. Light shining in darkness, and the darkness comprehending it not. That is an unusual story. I fancy . . ." and relapsed into silence again.

"What did you do?" Henry asked.

"I looked at it for a while," Captain Rushton said, "and then I went away. But I shut the window first."

"And put your arm right over the crosses?" Olivia asked.

"Right over them."

"And then you went away and left them blazing?" I finished.

"And left them blazing . . . left them the room to themselves."

Then the Stranger nodded.

"That is the right sort of story," he said. "Especially tonight. It was the light of Light, shining wondrously from the everlasting hills—from the altar-stone—from the rock of Calvary. The light of our faith may go out, but the light of Light eternally shines in the darkness. I understand that."

As no one said anything, he added: "When one is worn-out and good for nothing, one realises darkness . . . like a child left alone in a night-nursery . . . one waits for someone to come, with a light." Then, remembering he was not simply with the Philosopher and Olivia, he added more lightly: "I wait for Olivia's necklace and the Philosopher's shirt-front."

"My story is about light, too," said Mrs. Derwent, in a comfortable way, without waiting to be asked.

She was a good woman, who took the whole world with the large grain of salt of her own humour. Plump and placid, she was one of those people of whom others never suspect supernatural experiences, but who can generally tell more than one story. She smoothed her silken skirts, smiled at us all in a motherly way, and began.

"Not many years ago," she said, "a friend of mine came to me to ask if I would visit a certain cottage hospital for her while she was away on her holiday. She was the Catholic visitor, and there were two serious cases where the priest was likely to be needed, and one man to be coaxed back to his duties by a little friendly patience. I had a car, and it would only mean a run just out of town once a week. Rather against my will—for I am not fond of official visiting—I agreed. It would only be for a month. My friend gave me careful details about the patients I was to go and see, especially about the man who was to be coaxed back to his duties. And she added: 'By the way, there's a funny old man in the same ward who has quite lately come in. It was cancer of the tongue, poor old chap, and the tongue has been removed, and so, of course, he is not intelligible. He is rather touched, too, and always wants to discuss Catholicism with me. But as he is a Catholic—his wife entered his name in the register as R.C.—there is no need. I just smile and nod to him, and give him magazines and flowers and come away. You can't make out a word he says, and he talks at a great rate.'

"Well, my friend went out of town, and I entered on my new duties. I gave most of my time to the man who was a lapsed Catholic, because I was told that his illness was taking a serious turn. I found him not difficult to talk to, only over-worried with some public-house prejudices against the religion in which he had been born and of which he knew little except its annoying demand that he should go to Mass on Sundays, and make his Easter. The unintelligible old man in the same ward seemed a cheerful old fellow. The one word I could understand in his remarks was 'Catholic,' which I took to be the subject of his greatest pride, and on which I always congratulated him. 'A great grace, Mr. Smith,' I used to say, 'the greatest grace in the world.' And he would nod and jabber. The nurses said he was not quite all there.

"Nothing of any interest happened until the last week, when the other man—call him Brown—took a turn for the worse, and Sister told me that he seemed to be sinking. Of course, I sent for Father Lane, the parish priest. Sister told me that Brown had asked for him. I was unable to go myself on the day Sister 'phoned me this news, but Father Lane would do all that was necessary to help a soul to go to God, and I contented myself with offering up the trials of a garden fête and a dinner-party for his poor soul. But I was thinking of poor Brown so much that I opened the garden fête as badly as any woman could. Of course, I motored down to the hospital the first thing next day."

She paused, with the sense for effect that comes to a hardened teller of tales in nurseries—so, I think, this attic seemed to her.

But she found her audience all in order. The Philosopher had begun to give her his fullest attention the moment she mentioned that the old man had no tongue. Captain Rushton it would be impossible to imagine otherwise than entirely interested in anything. Henry, one felt, was quite ready to sum up; and Olivia, chin on hand, listened and looked on, seeing as well as hearing, leaving criticism to Henry. From the bed, keen as a child, the Stranger heard every word.

"Go on, please," he said. And Mrs. Derwent, who was unconsciously waiting for that familiar request, smoothed her lap again, and went on.

"When I arrived," she said, "I knew at once something had happened. Sister seemed positively fluttered, and she took me into her own little sitting-room, and shut the door. Brown was dead? No, Brown was a great deal better. But it wasn't about Brown. It was about Smith. She and nurse—could understand what Smith said!

"Then she began at the beginning. Father Lane had come at dusk on the previous day. She had taken him to the ward herself, and he had gone straight across to Brown's bed, round which the screens were drawn. He had brought the Blessed Sacrament with him, and had given Brown Viaticum and Extreme Unction. Then he had gone straight out of the ward again, when Brown was at peace with God and his own soul. They were both plain men, you know. Brown was sorry; Father Lane gave him the sacraments. I don't think they took much notice of each other beyond that.

"But when Sister had come back into the ward, she had found old Smith sitting up in bed, clasping a broken rosary, positively radiant, and saying something about a 'great light,' and that he wanted Father Lane. Bewildered, she had fetched Nurse, and they had both heard the same thing. Somehow, he could make them understand what he said quite easily. Now if you realise it, the word that had been intelligible to them before—Catholic—is comparatively easy without using the tongue."

The Philosopher had been trying it.

"Yes," he said, "you can mouth something quite like the word."

"But 'Father Lane' is nothing like so easy, and 'a great light' is almost impossible. Well, Sister took me to see the old man, and there he was, still with this broken rosary in his hand, still radiant about something. And I, too, could quite clearly understand that he had seen a great light and that he wanted Father Lane. He had refused to hand over his rosary for Sister or Nurse to take away and mend, but he gave it to me at once, apparently because he knew I was a Catholic, and so I sat and mended it by his bed, while he prattled on. You understand, his speech was nothing like ordinary, of course. But it was certainly intelligible, if one listened carefully. He made me understand that he had seen Father Lane come in at the door 'with a great light,' and that Father Lane had been behind the screens with Brown for a long while, and had then gone away. And that he believed in the Catholic Faith, and wanted Father Brown to bring him the 'great light.'

"You may imagine that I didn't know what to do. It all sounded the sort of unbalanced ramble that one so often hears, but there was the fact, the old man could make himself understood, a thing he had not been able to do previously, in spite of his continuous and valiant attempts to hold converse with everyone who passed his bed. Also, Sister said there was no light at all in the ward. No light had come with Father Lane. She was not a Catholic herself, and had only made such preparations as Father Lane asked for when he came.

"While we were wondering what to do, old Smith's wife arrived to see him, and from her we drew an explanation."

"Old Smith was not a Catholic, of course," the Stranger suggested.

"No, of course he wasn't. He was an agnostic, and had been one all his life. But when he had to go to this hospital, he had made his wife enter him as a Catholic in the register, saying he wanted to die in the Catholic religion. The broken old rosary was his badge, he considered, and I suppose he imagined would act as a disguise. Of course, being dumb, he was safe from any questions.

"You may imagine that I lost no time in fetching Father Lane. What he made of it I don't know. He had no fancy for fantastic stories. But he and old Smith understood each other well enough for him to baptise the old man without much delay. Sister said that it would be wise, because the doctors could not say how long old Smith might live. There were chances. . . . It might be any time, and quite sudden."

"And Father Lane brought him the Great Light," the Stranger said.

"Yes. The queer old chap did not live much longer. God had just given him light and speech to ask for the sacraments. From that time forth his rosary seemed never out of his hand, and he seemed to be in contact with Heaven. He died absolutely radiant. Sister and Nurse could talk of nothing else for weeks. He went to God as one would go to find one's youth and the joy of life. Brown recovered."

"And Sister and Nurse asked to be received?" From the Stranger again.

"Indeed they didn't," Mrs. Derwent said, shaking her head. "They were amazed and impressed beyond words, but I never heard that they became Catholics. They marvelled exceedingly, you know, but didn't care to question further."

"Only the old man saw the light," Olivia said, pensively.

The Stranger flung himself round on his pillows.

"Oh I know, I know," he said. "But it's the same Light that lighteneth every man who wants it. But everyone's striking brimstone matches in this wretched little world, so that nobody realises that except for that true Light we are completely in the dark.

Downstairs, there are plenty of pretty candles on the table, and I heard you chattering and laughing. But up here I knew it was towards night, and that I didn't know anything. And I prayed for someone to come and tell me a story."

"And there were we, entertaining and delaying the angels unawares," Henry said in his kindest, quietest tone. "For my part, I beg your pardon, old man."

His tone seemed to soothe the Stranger.

"I am a tiresome child who can't sleep," he said, "and you are all marvellously good to me."

"Of course, I am a heathen," Rushton said—and his voice was always listened to with pleasure wherever he spoke—"but I do think that when the Gospels talk about light they are at their best. I am often sent to church by the Embassy when I'm in Paris, and I always like what you call the 'last Gospel'—that first chapter of St. John. And while Mrs. Derwent was talking, I was thinking: 'This man came for a witness to give testimony of the light.'"

"I was thinking of that phrase in the psalms—one of the Compline psalms—'lumen vultus tui' ('the light of thy Countenance')," I said. "I love the Latin word 'lumen.' I wait for it in the *Credo* every Sunday—'lumen de lumine.' And in the *Nunc Dimittis*—'lumen ad revelationem gentium.' It suggests an aureole, a heavenly light, light coming through mist."

"Yes," the Philosopher said, musing. "Light—sunlight is life to us, but His life, lived in time, is the eternal light of men. 'O Oriens, splendor lucis aeternae!'. . . That was a good story, Mrs. Derwent."

"And now your Stranger ought to sleep," she said. "Will you sleep now, Mr. Stranger?"

"Probably not," he said, "but I think if Jane settled me with my thumb in my mouth, I might lie awake and blink at the stars quite happily."

So his visitors made their friendly adieux, their gracious tribute to his loneliness, and left him alone. He lay very patiently while

I straightened the room and set the windows wide and settled him until my last midnight visit.

Then at last I came to his bed and gave him his beads and the freshly eau-de-Cologned handkerchief.

"Is that all?" I asked. "A drink of water? A night-light?"

"No," he said. "Not a night-light. It's they who sit in darkness that see the great light. And I think I'll lie and look and see it all over again. Go to bed. God bless you," and he turned on his pillows, and looked towards the faint glimmer of the sanctuary-lamp through the far chapel window beyond the gardens.

THE SIXTH OF THE SEVEN TRUE STORIES

The Last Mercy

The Last Mercy

ITHERTO, the Stranger's visitors had come on errands of sympathy, to bring him grapes or flowers or a paper, or something from the pleasant world that was outside the attic. But things had changed. Now they came to get something from the other world in which the Stranger was already living. The darkness which had hung before his spirit for so many weary weeks, of what he called "this business of dying," had given place to a dawn that shone through his tired mind and through his breaking body like an almost visible aureole. Gone were his moods; instead, at whatever hour of the day or night he might need me, and in whatever condition of weakness or pain he might be, I was always greeted with a kind of divine nonsense—a tongue that none can speak except those who have heard the sound of children playing in the Kingdom of Heaven, and have seen the look in the eyes of the King as He watches them.

One evening Father Paul fetched me.

"Jane," he said, in a flustered tone, "do come. Between us, we spilt the teapot into his bed, and he got scalded, and everything's dripping, and it was his fault as much as mine."

The Stranger hailed me unperturbed.

"You'll have to restuff the mattress and wipe the bed-posts," he said. "No dry land. The raven came back to Noe and said: 'Not even the Himalayas fit to perch on.' I took the teapot to my heart."

That meant the painful business of moving him, with all the exhaustion that always followed it. But he lay there, gibing at Father

Paul, who fetched another mattress and knocked down everything within range in doing so, and coaxing me not to be stern with the pair of them, in a way that turned the whole affair into something amusing. When I would have exclaimed at the scalded patch on his thin chest, he put a finger to my lips, and went through a ridiculous dumb show to tell me how upset Father Paul would be if he knew the extent of the damage. And to distract that crestfallen cleric he began a tirade against his clumsiness.

"Look here," he said, wincing as I dressed the scald, "do leave that mattress alone, and stop waltzing about with it. It's by the fire to be aired, not to be given a little exercise. Here, come and help Jane turn me."

"You're not fit to be left alone," I said. "You're a couple of children. Give me that blanket."

"Well, Jane!" Father Paul expostulated. "He began it. He picked up the teapot and pointed it at me, and said: 'I tell you that was in the first year of the war,' and at every word he poured a little of it at me. And I tried to take it from him, and it went into the bed."

"What a version!" the Stranger countered. "You kept contradicting and saying that it was 1913, and I was merely emphasising my point . . ."

Somehow, I had whipped him safely into a dry environment, and I bade Father Paul rub his feet for awhile, because I was afraid of the effects of the shock of scalding.

"Very gently," I said. "Just the soles and the toes."

And reason enough, for the insteps were swollen and the skin was not whole. Father Paul looked up at me, and there were tears in his eyes; and then impulsively he put his lips to those insensitive and yet suffering feet, so like to those which were stretched ready for a soldier's mallet and an iron nail.

The Stranger was lying with closed eyes, and I busied myself with packing him round with warm bottles, and chafing his wrists and heart.

"What can I do now?" Father Paul asked, when I had wrapped the Stranger's feet warmly away.

The Stranger opened one eye. "Agree that it was the first year of the war," he said, and closed it again.

"What was the first year of the war?"

"That old Berry Mitchell made his century at Lord's."

"I don't," said Father Paul stubbornly. "I tell you why. I met old Berry last week, and we were saying . . ."

"Pcha!" said the Stranger, faint but unyielding, and I believe it would have begun all over again, but for the Philosopher's knock at the door.

"Can Henry and I come in?"

"Yes, and welcome," I said, "if you will stop these two from quarrelling. I want the Stranger to rest," and I told them what had happened. The Philosopher quiets any room he comes into, and Henry is the soul of truce except in the matter of politics. Peace was restored. The Philosopher discoursed idly upon the uses of tea, and Henry entered into the subject of cricket averages with the diplomacy of one promoting the League of Nations. And I, soothing the Stranger's wrist, with an unobtrusive finger on his pulse, smiled on them both. Presently Cambrilles scratched at the door, and before he had settled down on the hearthrug, there came Olivia, who unpinned the freesias on her coat and laid them in the Stranger's hand.

He welcomed her as heartily as he could, for he was happiest when his friends all came at once.

"Tired, Right Honourable Member?" he asked.

"Oh, yes," she said. "Glad to come up here."

"Tories quiet and the Red Flag waiting for a breeze?"

"I'm sick of the lot of them."

"Dear old Westminster," the Stranger said. "It's a long time since I heard a debate. But I've heard a good many. Yes, you look tired, my dear. Won't things go as you want them to?"

"If seven maids with seven mops mopped it for generations it wouldn't be tidy."

"I know," he said. "And you want to build Jerusalem in England's green and pleasant land, and it won't even be pleasant, and it's far too green. Well, let's change the subject for a bit." He talked to his visitors now as though they were children, and somehow they liked it. "I have just been having a tea-bath"—and he told Olivia the story. "I don't know what the discussion began about," he said in conclusion.

"About that day I had tea with Berry," Father Paul said. "I was going to tell you ..."

"Oh, yes, something queer. You got as far as: 'I've never done such a thing in my life before, and I don't know if I was right.'"

Henry glanced at his wife.

"Take your hat off, darling," he said. "We are going to have a story."

Father Paul protested.

"No," he said, "there is no beginning and end to it, and it isn't the story for a sick room, exactly."

"You mean it isn't the story for the others," the Stranger said, "because you were going to tell me before we had that little difference of opinion." He pulled the sheet cosily under his chin. "Get on with it, Reverend Father."

After some demur, Father Paul told what he had to tell.

"I was calling on old Berry one afternoon last week," he said, "and his rooms are on Campden Hill, you know. It was a filthy, skiddy day, and we were wondering whether it was too wretched to get his car out and come down here to see the Stranger, when all of a sudden, I saw a bus skid and a woman knocked down and swept under the wheels. The first thing that flashed into my mind was that she might be a Catholic, and it was certain death."

He looked at the others, and I knew that he was omitting any dreadful details.

"So ... I don't know whether I was right, but I gave her conditional absolution ... from the window. Then, of course, I rushed down. But the police wouldn't let me through because she was dead, and they said she wore no medals or anything. She was a woman of thirty or forty. There was a doctor with her. He had been in the bus. I am afraid it's a pointless, morbid thing to tell. Only it was curious . . . my being at the window."

"And more curious still that I can finish the story," the Philosopher said, with a note in his voice that makes whatever he says sound like a *Te Deum*. "That doctor was my friend Verney, and he was dining with me that night, and the conversation turned on casualties. He told me his experience that day, and he told me one fact which, in the light of Father Paul's story, is all that matters. The woman lived five minutes after he got to her. She was alive, then, when Father Paul gave her absolution.

"And that is not all. You know I have been in town a good bit lately. I have been with a little old woman whose heart is broken and whose faith has nearly broken. For twenty years she has been praying for one thing—that God would not let her only daughter, who had given up the practice of her religion, die without absolution. And last week her daughter was knocked down by a motor bus. . . . Yes, on Campden Hill. She was a woman of thirty-eight."

"You'll go up to town first thing tomorrow, won't you?" Father Paul said, "and tell the old lady?"

"No," the Philosopher said. "I shall go now. Look me up a train, please, Jane."

Olivia leant forward.

"Wait just half an hour," she said, "and Bridgett will have finished his meal, and be back for orders, and you can have my car. Do. I'd like you to. There isn't a train until later."

"What about you?"

"I can go by train, easily," she said.

"Bless you," the Stranger said. "Pagan you may be, but you do understand. And if I hadn't upset the tea, you'd never have heard that story, Philosopher."

His eyes were shining, and yet his pulse was as tranquil as though he were asleep. Yet he was very much awake. So much awake that he hushed the others.

"The ways of God," he said; "you have time to study them—all of you. The Mind of God. The thoughts of God. The warp of His eternal purpose and the woof of all that He permits to happen— the warp of Being and the woof of Becoming—making the perfect weaving of the eternal plan. Watch that. That is life. That is as the angels see it. That is the truth about this world. Watch the whole marvellous pageantry of the redemption of a single human soul. It begins two thousand years ago in time, with a man nailed helpless to a cross, and it goes on down the years until the moment that a great petrol-driven invention pins that creature down to an asphalte roadway. And for that moment it has everything ready—a priest to raise his hand at the bidding of that nailed hand, and give the pardon that nailed hand had won by its transfixion; a doctor to witness that the woman was alive to receive the pardon; the Philosopher to know the old mother. And all because that old woman prayed, and God foreknew that she would pray. No, rather that God urged her to pray, and she prayed because her prayer was to be answered. And even after that, how He kept the good news safe between so many witnesses, until the old mother's faith had been tried enough to win for herself the everlasting joy of having trusted God when He seemed to slay her by breaking her heart. It is all perfect. He can't do anything that is not perfect, and most tender and beautiful . . . the Ancient Beauty. All *that* prepared before the creation of the world . . . the Lamb slain before the foundation of the world . . . for one soul that wilfully ran away from Him."

He had lifted himself up on his pillows, and I let him be. He was radiant but not excited, and joy would not harm him. Besides, he was talking to us all, and it was good for *us* to be there.

"And look at it from the soul's point of view. A wasted life. She may have gained the whole world, but she had lost her soul. But her old mother found it for her again. That's what I see. There was no more time to do anything fine and great for God. No more time to serve Him. No time to do all a soul is capable of. No more time to be brave. No more pride of strength. No more gallantry. The soul could do no more for God, but God could still do all for the soul, because in that moment every instinct was afraid, and the soul must have given the cry that the heart of God was waiting to hear. Don't you see, if we let God have us in all the glory of our youth and strength, flinging the pride of life under His feet, like a Sir Walter Raleigh's cloak with a *beau geste*, and putting his yoke on our lithe shoulders instead, then we come to *find* our life. But if we only fall a prey to that Divine Love when we are too weak to be wilful, we only have time to find one thing—our need of Him. And even that is a happy ending, because He has found us and we have found our pitiful mistake. We have found holy poverty. Because, you know"—he seemed to be talking to the whole world— "even the grace to know our need, we could not have merited after a life of wilfulness. Some faithful creature, who loved us better than we knew, had been praying—an old cook, or a nun we criticised as being as stiff as the pie-frill of her coif, or the stupid parish priest whose collars were dirty under his red face. We have lost the whole world—lost our chance to praise and serve God—but someone has gained our soul for us. One of God's maids-of-all-work picked it out of the dust-bin. We have never possessed our own soul. We threw it away because it was a bother. But someone bought it with prayer and patience and gave it to God. Bought it with His Precious Blood, of course. And now He possesses it, and all is well with us. We have nothing—no pride. We are utterly at peace. I don't think we say so much 'God be merciful to me, a sinner,' as 'God be merciful to me, a fool.' Such a waste of time. To run away from God." He laughed, a queer ecstatic laugh. "How abysmally silly!"

And then he folded his hands, and was very quiet.

Henry stirred in his chair. "I am the only one left out," he said. "That won't do. I shall drive you, Philosopher, if I may."

"Yes," the Philosopher said dreamily, "that would be quite right." Silence fell again.

"There's only one thing," he said: "if the whole story is based on a premiss we have no right to make, namely that the woman was in a state to receive absolution, that she was sorry and wanted it."

"Attrition is enough," Father Paul said. "And in an awful death like that, they would be almost bound to . . ."

"Nevertheless," the Philosopher said, "we cannot know that. We must take it on faith."

"Like true love, and the origin of matter, and the existence of God," the Stranger said, "we must believe it with the great act of faith we make when we believe our five senses. Faith—the first principle of finite intelligence. Poof! Who but God sent Father Paul to that window? And who but God, the Second Person of the Blessed Trinity, said: 'Whosoever sins you remit, they are remitted'?

"'I believe all the Son of God has spoken.
Than Truth's own word there is no truer token.'"

"Oh yes," Olivia said, unconsciously, and I echoed it.

"That's all right," the Philosopher said, getting up. "I wanted all those acts of faith. I'll go now, if you are ready, Henry."

THE SEVENTH OF THE SEVEN TRUE STORIES

"…And Myrrh"

"...And Myrrh"

HE FIRE BLAZED among its pine logs, and the candles threw reflections of their steady flames into the polished surfaces of cupboards and settles. I sat in my rocking-chair, listening to the impetuous wind outside coming over the woods to shake our windows and to remind us that it was very safe and cosy in the attic. The Philosopher sat on the left-hand side of the hearth, and Henry sat on the right side, and beside him on the high-backed settle sat Olivia in a golden ball-dress, waving a fan of paradise plume.

It was Father Paul's birthday, and he had saved his cake until Henry and Olivia came. There it was, with twenty-eight little candles blazing away on it. And we sat sipping the Philosopher's best cowslip wine, drinking his health. In the four-post bed, the Stranger was sitting up on his pillows, enjoying it all, and watching the candlelight through his little glass of wine. His hands seemed no less transparent, and happiness shone in his eyes. He loved such an evening. Cambrilles lay on the settle beside the Philosopher. He had accepted a very large portion of cake, and was now rather a cynic than an epicurean. When spoken to, he opened one eye. When offered more cake, he shut it.

"He refuses it like a Methodist elder refusing strong drink," said Father Paul. "Watch him raise one paw and put it from him! He's a prudent little dog, a bit late with his prudence."

Henry was pulling away at his pipe. He had made a speech that afternoon which had exactly caught his audience's enthusiasm. We were all pleased with the success, and with what the Prime

Minister had said afterwards. But Henry was best pleased with the fact that he had got it over and done with. He was like a boy let out of school. His holiday task would be to take Olivia to her ball, but he could stay where he was for another hour or so. Besides, Olivia was very presentable.

"Isn't she nice?" he asked us suddenly, pointing at his wife with his thumb. "I do think she looks nice. Not pretty, perhaps, but so clean and tidy—such an honest face."

Olivia placidly went on knitting a sock for one of her sons.

"You are in the mood to think the whole world rather jolly," she said. "Youth with its first achievement, and a little cowslip wine. Henry! If you ruffle my hair, I shan't do it again!"

The Stranger chuckled at them. He was in Henry's mood. He knew that it was for his benefit that Olivia had dressed early, and was trailing golden tissue over the polished boards of the attic. Henry, too, had come upstairs three at a time to tell him that he had "done himself rather uncommonly well." Even the cake had been saved to add its candles and pink icing to the festiveness of the occasion.

"Jane," he said, "this room must feel that it is a nursery again. I should like to dance a minuet with Olivia."

"I could play a jig," Father Paul said, a little drowsily, from the depths of a chair, whence all that was visible was his head and his knees, with his hands clasped round them.

"Christmas is near enough to be infectious," I said. "That's what we are all feeling in the air."

Cambrilles snuggled up to the Philosopher, and gave a sigh and a sniff of perfect content.

"It seems to me," the Philosopher said, "that Heaven will be transcendently like this. We shall certainly be in this kind of a mood—absolutely ourselves and absolutely at home."

Olivia asked: "Is this absolutely myself?"

"No, but not far from it. To be absolutely oneself is to be perfectly what one is potentially. You are doing something for one of your children, Henry is in love with you, you are looking beautiful, and you are decking this attic with yourself which is what you were made beautiful for. And you know why we love you, and . . ."

"Why do I love Olivia?" Father Paul said drowsily. "She took a snapshot of me being furious with the Philosopher, and I didn't know I loved her . . . at all."

"Yes you do," Olivia said soothingly. "You love me because I remind you of a green plum stone, with a little of the plum sticking to it. You told me so."

"So I did," he said. "And I said you were also like the duck-pond with the sun on it. You may laugh, Henry, but she is. It's a very complimentary simile."

"*I* love you for the way you carry a baby under one arm," the Stranger said. "And for the way you contradict Henry. But we all interrupted the Philosopher. What were you going to say?"

"You didn't interrupt: you illustrated. Every human being receives from another human being that impression of which he is capable."

"You mean," Henry said, "that, not understanding the matter of my speech this afternoon, you only appreciate the fact that apparently I was a heavy success because the Prime Minister . . ."

"I mean," said the Philosopher, "that *I* appreciate in you your taste in tobacco because I want some tobacco. Lend me your pouch, please. And the only companionableness is appreciation. Henry, I understand, is a plus-four, or something, at golf. Now, having no use for golf, I have no use for that ability of Henry's. But Father Paul has. And being all things to all men, which is the community life of the Kingdom of Heaven, really consists in being to everyone something that he has a use for. Therefore, to go back a long way, one is most consciously oneself when various potentialities of oneself are being of use to various people. Therefore, we are all in rather a heavenly mood tonight."

Olivia nodded.

"Hark at the rain!" the Stranger said. "More like sleet. So our potentialities are what the New Testament calls talents. But can you call those most loveable things a potentiality—Father Paul's way of scudding downstairs and saying 'Sorry' to Cambrilles when he lands on top of him, and Olivia's way of tucking Remi under one arm, and . . . and so on?"

"I think they are the very essence—the manifestation of the very essence—of some potentiality. For instance, Father Paul gets to the bottom of things in a discussion in just the same way, and has just the same human, unnecessary sympathy for the man he 'downs.' It is his talent for going straight to the ground of things. But to dissect is to destroy. One would as soon pull a flower to pieces, and botanise over a lily to find out why the Church loves lilies. Like flowers, these are characteristics—they are symbols of some state of mind, as flowers are of the Mind of God."

"That's reassuring to people who wonder whether their mother's way of holding her sewing will survive the general resurrection," Henry said. "And we all know that it's things like that we want to be certain we shall see again."

"I once heard of a nun who saw our Lord," I said. "And I was told that her most cherished memory of the seeing seemed to be that He had a little way of pushing His hair from His face with His left hand."

The wind thundered against the windows under the gables.

"I should be impelled to believe a vision like that," the Philosopher said. "That is what the Incarnation means."

After a moment he added:

"All but the mystics are astray. Heaven is the quintessential bliss of what our inmost soul knows would be home to us. It is not a haven only, but the desired haven. There we shall find, not a heap of crowns, but something more like the contents of the secret drawer—not withered, but in the glory of eternal youth. The Beatific Vision won't be an amazing surprise, but something so exactly what we longed for in the depths of our heart, that eternity will be the endless coming true of the dim, human dream of fifty or eighty little years. Meister Eckhart says: *'God is near us, but we are far from him. God is within: we are without. God is at home: we are in a far country.'* For when we deny our own best hopes, we deny God, and when we lose our spirit's secret faith, we lose our soul. I wish I could preach that. Calvinism and Jansenism have sent uncountable spirits into the hell which is the antithesis of home. Tauler says that the contemplative attains to finding a place where there is *'only God and nothing strange.'* That is what one says to a frightened child, weeping in the night. 'There is nobody here except mother.' 'Only God, and nothing strange.' We are content with a world of appearances and happenings—until we suddenly wake up, in a sweat of fear, to know that we don't know what it all means. But unless the mystics of the world's history have united in a tremendous inheriting and passing on of a lie—unless our spirit lies about what it is crying for, that is the reply we are listening for—coming from the heart under which we were conceived. 'It is all right. You were wandering in a dream. But you knew whom to cry for. You are at home, in your own place. There is only God, and nothing strange.'"

The trees hushed round the house, and the wind wailed. An imperceptible draught blew the blue lamp before our Lady's shrine in the corner of the room.

"Are we in our own places?" I asked him.

"Certainly. Your own place is the niche your potentialities make for you. Circumstances are appearances. Those are of little importance. They are clay, shaped by the divine purpose and your ability to make something of them. Their reason is only to bring out the best in you. Your own place is something eternal, round which time and temporal appearances pass like mist. Your face is your fortune. Your place is your purpose. And," he added, "those things we love in this world are things that we recognise. They are keepsakes of a tryst with that of which they are the manifestation. And believe me, you will never be nearer to communion with the Mind of God than when you believe that the language in which you can best understand Him, and in which He will make you understand all you desire to know, is the unutterable language of the heart. Remember, that with whatever unimaginable and terrible love the Infinite God loves the planets and the uncharted world beyond our knowledge of worlds, it is with a human heart that He loves our human personalities. He loves us as He made us to want to be loved. He understands that which He has made. We are strange to ourselves, but we are not strange to God who made us; and the God who made us cannot be strange to us. He must be our oldest, dearest home. He must know our wants. Our worship of Him can only be a blissful agony of adoration of His comprehension."

The logs embered, loosening their glowing opals of tinder into the blaze. The candles burnt straight like the hands of angels in prayer. The strange six of us . . . and the dog seemed poised in a little ark above the darkness and storm below. The Philosopher had spoken as he rarely spoke.

It was the Stranger who added to what he had said.

"I'll tell you a story to help you believe that," he said, very tranquilly. "I have never told you a story, and you have told me many. I never intended to tell this to a living soul, but I give it to you . . . as a keepsake. It is the most precious thing I have to give."

With an effort, he stretched out his hand for the little glass, and moistened his mouth with wine. Then he folded his hands again, and went on:

"It is a story about the woman I loved. My early marriage, as you know, was a failure. Many years later, I met the only woman who could have given me perfect happiness. She was a Pole, and, when I met her, considered the greatest beauty in Warsaw. Her name was Catherine. She was married to a man whose infidelity was notorious: the proudest, hardest man who ever fought for his country. He was never in Poland, and I never set eyes on more than his portrait. I did not need to tell Catherine that I should never marry another woman. We understood each other perfectly, and she trusted me absolutely. I don't think the gossips even suggested that we loved each other, but she was all I desired in this world, and when we parted, she said: 'Life has given me more than I dreamed. God knew and sent me more than I dared hope. Now let us do His will until death.' I can hear her saying it now. I wish you could have known her. She was perfect from head to heel, with a dark Grecian head and white skin and the most beautiful eyes that sorrow ever hid in. She dressed very quietly, but everything that belonged to her was fragrant of a perfume—a French perfume with the strange name of '*Myrrhe et Lis.*' Well, one day I was in some country place in Poland and she was in Warsaw. I was trying to make up my mind what to do—whether to return to England or to go back to Arabia. The little country town I happened to be in was a dreary little place. One night, I went to church, to try and get the grace to know the will of God. She knew I was occupied with this question, and I was longing to have her there, just to advise me in her loved voice. I knew she would consider nothing but the will of God, and how best to fulfil it. In church I prayed for a time, but in vain. I came away troubled and heavy-hearted, unable to see what to do for the best, doubting everything but my love for Catherine. I walked until I came near the railway, a dreary part of the town, away from houses and quite deserted. And there, as I trudged along, suddenly I smelt Catherine's perfume. And as I stood still, unable to believe my sense, which declared to me that it was the one perfume I couldn't possibly mistake, there came clear into my mind an answer to my difficulties. I saw exactly what to do. It was to be England, not Arabia. And I saw clearly the details of what to do next. There I stayed, breathing in the air as though it were not the flat air of a town, and blowing over the coal-trucks in a railway station. And there I understood. God had sent the light, as it were, *wrapped up in her fragrance,* in that scent that was a symbol of her personality, which spoke of her as a vision of her could hardly have done. The next morning I had a letter from her, saying she had been wishing she could be with me to help me decide, and that she had been praying especially for me. And so I came to England."

He added, a minute later:

"It wasn't a scent that came from a passing train, you know. The station was deserted. It was late at night. Nor had I a handkerchief or anything of hers. I could not bear to smell that scent unless it told me she was present. But since then, every Christmas, she has sent me a few lines, and the paper has smelt very faintly of that scent. That will explain any scent you might notice among my papers. That is all. That is divine courtesy. So you need not be afraid He does not understand human things."

He signed to me to move some of his pillows. He was tired.

"I followed the light that I had then until it brought me here," he said. "So you can take it that He meant me to tell you that story."

One by one, we said thank you.

We did not feel inclined to talk after that. The Philosopher sat quiet in his corner, thinking. Father Paul did not stir. But I had to give the Stranger his medicine, and refill his hot water bottle. And Henry, looking at his watch, said they must go.

"Good-night, Stranger dear," Olivia said. "We will treasure your keepsake. I shall come back in the morning and tell you about the ball, and if I was good and if Henry was good to me."

"I shall say: 'Keep you safe till morning light,'" he replied, smiling at her. "You deserve to be happy. And you remind me of Catherine tonight. She used to wear gold. Say good-night to the children for me. Good-night, Henry. You are doing nothing more for Brighter England tonight? I'd like to take a hand with you. I wasn't always such a crock."

Henry moved a pillow with which the Stranger was fumbling.

"I'll tell you what I really *said*, in the morning," he promised. "I'll come up here when you are alone. I wish I needn't go now, but I expect you're tired."

"Yes," he said. "I am. Wrap Olivia up well. Good-night."

Father Paul followed them downstairs. I had only to settle the Stranger for sleep. The Philosopher was taking night-duty.

He let me set him in order, without talking, but when I had given his beads into his hand, he bade me open his writing case, and give him a little packet that was done up in oiled silk.

"Catherine's letters," he said. "Each one means a year. And now, go to bed, Jane. I don't want this nursing to ruin your health. I am keeping you from London and your writing. You may write that story, if you like—if you think it would be of comfort to anyone."

"I will," I said. "I think it would. But are you sure I may?"

"It is all I have, you know," he said, with his funny smile. "Youth and beauty are gone, and riches I never had. But that is my pearl of great price. Good-night, Jane. God bless you"—and to my surprise, he kissed my hand.

"Don't," I said. "There are all too many books, but I love nursing."

"Go to bed," he said, waving his thin hand. "It is late." I saw him smile at me—his rare smile—as I closed the door.

·   ·   ·   ·   ·

The Philosopher woke me before the dawn, sitting on the edge of my bed, with a candle in his hand, showing me his face. I stared at him.

"Oh no," I said. "Not that! Not while I was asleep!"

"Father Paul was with him," he replied gently. "No one else. Put on your dressing-gown, and come and see him."

When I went into the attic, the Philosopher had lit all the candles. Father Paul, in white cotta and stole, was kneeling by the bed.

He raised his head. He was very pale and his eyes full of awe. It was he—I realised—little more than a boy, who had been the one to go the last lonely steps of the way to eternity with the Stranger.

"It was all right," he said. "The Philosopher came for me and I gave him Viaticum. Then he sent the Philosopher away, and when I suggested fetching you, he said: 'No. I must be alone.' I told him the Philosopher had gone to the chapel to pray for him, and he told me to thank him. 'And thank them all,' he said. Then he lay for a long while praying, and bade me say the *Magnificat* and the *Te Deum*, in thanksgiving for all God's mercies.

"'I can't remember my sins,' he said. 'Only His dear mercies.' And when I was saying, 'Dominus Deus Sabaoth,' he opened his eyes and said 'Jesus' and 'Catherine' and . . . and sighed . . . as though he couldn't bear any more happiness or pain . . . and he was dead."

I looked at the face on the pillow, the strong chin and deep eyes with their heavy lids. The Philosopher and Father Paul had crossed his hands on his breast, and in them lay the crucifix and Catherine's letters. I bent over him—the Stranger who was a stranger no longer—to kiss the still fingers. Faint from the bundle of letters came a fragrance unique and beautiful—myrrh and lilies.

L'ENVOI

"We rest
Aware that thou art better than our best."

RODEN NOEL.

ODD JOB'S

An Odd Book of Odd Stories

CONTENTS

TO

SCUTTLES

WHO LIKED THESE STORIES

ABOUT

BARNABAS JOB

THIS SLENDER BOOK OF THEM

IS

DEDICATED

WITH AFFECTION

Introducing Barnabas

"Each soul of the beloved of the King has its own secret with Him."—ST. BERNARD.

ODD JOB'S

Introducing Barnabas

"THE HEEL'S COME off my shoe, and I've got to walk two miles, and they tell me you can mend it while I wait."

Standing framed in the low doorway of his tumble-down cottage, the little old man seemed to Philippa to have been built up in that game called "Head, Body and Legs," which children play on winter evenings, drawing a head, folding down the paper and passing it on to the next player to have a body added, and then legs, until the unfolded whole shows the queerest of portraits. This little old man had the smooth parted hair of an evangelical minister, the eyes of a contemplative saint, the snub nose of a boy, the lean body of a vagabond and the bow legs of an ostler; his hair grey, his eyes grey, his cardigan grey, his breeches corduroy, his neckerchief scarlet and petunia, his face sunburnt, his teeth crooked but surprisingly white when he smiled as he was smiling now, his hand on the doorpost wrinkled, but long-fingered and stout-wristed with a capable humorous thumb.

"Ah," he said, oracularly, "I can mend most things for them as waits, but most won't wait. Set in the porch 'ere, missy, and take it off."

"Thanks very much," said Philippa Lovel. "Bad luck, wasn't it?"

"Not for me," he answered drily. "I shall charge yer fourpence. I'll fetch me tools. I works outside when fine. Yer don't mind 'ammering?"

"Not at all," she replied, in her level, conventional voice, but he had disappeared, taking her shoe with him.

What an odd old person! Philippa looked about her. This front garden was square, sloping down the hillock on which the cottage was built, to the cart-track which the villagers called a road. It had flower-beds round the sides of each little lawn to left and right of the path that led up to the front door, flower-beds brimming over with red daisies, clumps of primulas of every colour from yellow to purple, narcissus, arabis and various perennials waiting for the summer. In one corner there were grape hyacinths, and the leafy remains of scyllas at the foot of an ivy-covered tub, from which reigned a dilapidated statue of Our Lady, evidently lately revived with Reckitt's Blue, applied with more generosity than skill. Philippa, who had a very fastidious taste in art, and who might have been an artistic prig but for a generous sense of humour, could not help smiling at it. The hedges round the cottage were of hawthorn, now vividly in leaf. High overhead in the sunshine a lark hung singing.

The owner of the garden reappeared with a wooden bench, and sitting astride it, so as to use it for a seat as well as work-table, he began to search diligently in his pocket for suitable nails.

"Now, I don't remember 'aving seen yer face before," he began, as impudently as a cock robin. "A town lady?"

"More or less," said Philippa, with a glint of amusement in her deep blue eyes.

"And your name, missy?"

"My name is Philippa."

"I'm not surprised," he said. "Yer takes six-and-three-quarters, and," regarding her foot over the top of the spectacles he had put on to do his work, "yer could easy squeeze into a six-and-a-quarter. Low 'eels. Good strong leather. None of these 'igh-'eeled, brown-paper-soled names for you—Gladys or May. Named after one of the 'Oly Apostles, like a Christian. Sensible sort."

Somehow, it did not sound impertinent as he said it, with the soft and serious inflexions of his voice. But although sensible was an adjective that suited Philippa Lovel admirably, she was sensible enough not to like it very much, for she was a very feminine person for all her stout shoes.

"I hope not," she said.

His sudden laughter was deep and unexpected.

"O, deary-o, you 'opes not! Married, are you?" (For there was a grey doeskin glove on her left hand.)

But Philippa had been questioned enough.

"Five times," she said soundly. "And I have thirty-nine children. And who are you?"

The cobbler took some tacks out of his mouth before he laughed again, and shook his head as though to reprimand himself for having merited to be called to order.

"Me? I'm old Job. Barnabas Job. Called Odd Job because I'm a bit foolisher and a bit wiser than most. J.O.B. Job. Named after the man after God's own 'eart, who didn't like the talk of his neighbours. More do I."

"Still," said Philippa, "humanity evidently interests you."

"Ah," he replied, "'umanity when it's 'uman; but not when it's a parish," and he hammered with gusto. "And 'ow did this 'appen?" he asked, indicating the heel.

"I tore it off in the quarry," she said. "I have been tramping cross-country."

"Ketchin' specimens?"

"No."

"Savin' time?"

"No."

"Then it was solitood yer was after. Yer fancied yer'd do a bit of thinkin'."

Any immediate reply would have passed unheard, for before the words were out of his mouth, he began to hammer furiously; and when he ceased, his shrewd wide-set eyes regarding her over those crooked spectacles were so void of ignorant curiosity and so full of benignity, that Philippa nodded. She could not help smiling at him.

"Ah," said Odd Job. "I often fancies I'll do a bit of thinkin' time and again. Settles one, kind of. There's nobody round 'ere as does it. Windmills or water-butts they might be, for all the thinkin' they do, pore souls."

"What do you think about?" asked Philippa.

"Life," said Odd Job, "and love." And he hammered furiously again. "Yes," he continued, when he laid down his hammer, and began to search for a knife. "Life I thinks about. I've seen a good bit of life, for I was on the roads until I was turned fifty. And always readin'. You'd be a lady that went in for readin', I fancy?"

"I read books and I bind them," said Philippa. "Book-binding is my profession."

She had realised how precious the least item of fresh interest must be to this active-brained little cobbler in this tiny Sussex village, and the warm-heartedness that was far more characteristic of Philippa than her slightly stiff manner, had conquered.

"Yer do, do yer?" said Barnabas Job. "Now, that's interesting. I mind once, when I was on the roads, I got a job to mend the 'ymn-books of Bethsaida Chapel, East Totton. I mended eighty. Chapel-keeper give me sixpence and a cup-er-cocoa. Then something give inside me. I coco-nut shies them back at him, and then the cocoa, and I opens his mouth and give him the sixpence to swaller. But I was Alfred Jenkins then. Pore soul. Never bin but half alive. Chapel-keeperin's liverish and makes a man terrible near."

"What do you mean about being Alfred Jenkins?" asked Philippa, who was now hoping he would not hurry with her shoe. She wanted more of this conversation. "Did you change your name?"

"Ar. Baptism," said Mr. Job. "Catholic I am now, praise God."

"So am I," said Philippa. "But one doesn't change one's sur-name in Baptism, even if one is a convert."

"I 'ad to," said Mr. Job. "The devil would 'ave 'ad me if I 'adn't."

"But why?"

"Because of the way I saw things in the catechism," the old man said, frowning sternly at his work. "You see, my dear, I was walkin' from London to . . . anywheres. I must-a met a lot of people, but the only one as met *me* was Father Boneyvencher. I was a bit scared of monks then, never 'avin' met any. But 'e was different. They all are—all as I've met. Well, 'e was readin' a book in 'is garden, brown frock and rope and all. And I stares at 'im, and 'e gives me good evening, and one thing led to another and we got talking, and at last 'e 'as me in for a bit of something, and a bed in the 'ayloft, and the next day I does a job in his garden, 'im being no good more'n a child with a pruning knife. And there, somehow, I stayed. And after a bit I got asking questions, and blowin' the organ, and then I saw how things were, and the grace of faith came to me. Well, then, of course, I 'ad to learn about the old Adam and the new Adam; and I said to Father Boneyvencher, 'Father,' I says, 'I've 'ad me old Adam a long time and I'm through with 'im. I'll be-gin to be somebody else.' 'Yes,' said Father Boneyvencher, 'you'll begin to be Christ.' 'No,' I says, 'I wouldn't know where to begin doing that, but I'll begin to be somebody 'E'll be glad of.' Father Boneyvencher tries to make me see about being Christ the Lord, but I couldn't. So at last 'e says, 'Very well,' 'e says, 'you begin to be a comfort to 'Im and a comfort to pore souls in this 'ard world.' So 'e baptised me Barnabas, because 'e said that was the name for a son as 'll be a comfort to you. And then I couldn't go on being Jenkins. Jenkins was no good. 'E was the rest of the old Adam that had been kind of drowned in baptism, so to speak. So I calls meself Job, because I'd 'ad a powerful lot of trouble, and likely to 'ave more. And then Job was a man after God's own 'eart, you see. Besides, as

Father Boneyvencher says to me, 'Barnabas,' he says, 'preach you can't, but you can do odd jobs.' So then I comes here to do odd jobs over beyond at the convent and in the village to make a bit extra. I put up the board . . . But you wouldn't have seen it, coming over from the quarry, for it faces the village. *Odd Job's.* That's what I puts. And you see I mends a pramberlater, and shoes, and makes coffins, and 'elps with the 'arvest, and I couldn't tell you 'ow many things I don't do. That's my vo-cation. Odd jobs. And I reckon it's a comfort to God A'mighty to 'ave somebody like that, for odd jobs, and it certainly is a comfort to the village."

He glanced over his spectacles to have this opinion confirmed. Philippa smiled back at him.

"Of course it is," she said.

Appreciation and understanding were the wine of life to Barnabas Job—wine which rarely came his way. His face lit up and broke into wrinkles of pleasure until he looked like a winter pippin.

"Yer shoe's done," he said. "But could yer fancy a cup-er-tea?"

He was evidently anxious to prolong this heartening visit.

"It would save my life," said Philippa.

"Then bide there," nodded Mr. Job, his face crumpling again with pride and pleasure. He bore off his tools, and shuffled into the well-like stillness of his kitchen.

Philippa put on her shoe. Far over the valley the sun was golden, glorious and kind. She could hear Barnabas Job washing his hands in the sink. So he thought his vocation was to be a comfort to his Maker. She thought of the Blessed Trinity, eternally sufficient to Themselves, in the bliss of Their Being. She could imagine Them deigning to be praised by the Carthusians, whose monastery spire stood out against the blue distance, but Odd Job!

"Kittles praises the Lord much like a lark do, if you notice," said Mr. Job, appearing suddenly with a black teapot and a cup and saucer, pink-rimmed and large. "Charitable things, too, kittles. Always doin' a kindness. And when they do bile over on the cat, no unkindness intended. Only the laws of science, so to speak. Could you fancy a little watercress, missy?"

He was off again across his garden to the brook, dodging a sandy cat, who ran at him, wishing to rub against his boots with the ecstatic affection of its kind, and, arriving too late, rolled languorously on the gravel path in the sun, and washed itself impulsively.

Philippa was tired in a pleasant way from her long tramp, and tired in a way that was not pleasant. It was a tiredness of the heart and will. Duty was pulling one way, her artist-nature another. Next month, the patched and mended wretch of a man that had once been Alastair Graeme was coming out of the last hospital where there had been any hope of doing more for him. Blind, helpless, nerve-wrecked, he was like some sad puppet made in dim likeness of the man who had been engaged to Philippa in 1916. He had prayed to die. He had, at the same time, done everything in his power to help the surgeons to make him a useful member of society and a possible husband for Philippa. Finally, yesterday, he had asked Philippa to give him back her ring—that half hoop of dark rubies that they had chosen together so blissfully. "You must never see the thing again," he had said. "Take it off and give it to me, please. Forget it! Go on with your work. Be busy and happy. That is what I want." And all the time, louder than any word he said, was the cry of his whole wracked being to be taken to a new home and tended by a woman who was not a nurse in a starched apron, but Philippa, the Philippa he adored. Before she could give him any kind of answer—even the answer of hesitation—his doctor had been shown in, and Philippa had made her escape. Today she had walked miles trying to decide what she would do. She had been deeply in love with Alastair. But these long years had changed him from a striding giant of a fellow at her beck and call, to a thin form in a flat wheelchair, with almost blind eyes behind black glasses, and blacker moods of depression in which even she could do little to rouse him. If she married him, she saw, with her own particular prudence and wisdom, she must do it now, without hesitation, and must put everything else out of her mind for ever. But could she stand years of tending him, unrepaid by any real companionship, to give her youth to him, and to lose him probably just when the best of life was gone, just when a woman most needs a home and a husband and children? Those black moods! Would they yield to the whole-time care which she could give him as his wife? Or would they win, and would she become a mere drudge of a woman, old before her time, worn out and impatient with him?

"Now," said Barnabas Job. "That's the bread and butter, and that's the watercress, and raspberry jam, and there we are. Nice strong tea, and a good spoonful of sugar and a drop er-cream, and now help yerself, missy."

Philippa's preference was for unsugared China tea and wafers of bread and butter, but somehow this very large cup of red tea was comfortable. She dipped watercress into the coarse moist salt, folded the long slices of bread and butter, and smiled at Mr. Job.

"You are very kind," she said.

"One of my jobs," said her host, "and when I'm doing one of my jobs, I'm onbearable happy. Onbearable. That's vo-cation, Father Boneyvencher used to say. Here, Pansy, lad, here's a saucer of tea!"

A black jowl projected under a privet hedge beside the cottage, and, at Mr. Job's words, two black eyes became visible, and then the head and neat body of a cocker-spaniel.

"Dog-pup," said Mr. Job. "But 'is face made me have to name 'im Pansy. Jest like the black part of a pansy."

Pansy wriggled ingratiatingly up to his master, and then sniffed Philippa's outstretched hand.

"Minds a baby beautiful, 'e does," said Barnabas Job. "Jest licks its face round and round if it cries. Pansy's a good little feller. Knows how to 'elp me, 'e does, don't yer, bad lad?"

"Tell me more about your vocation," Philippa asked.

Mr. Job had seated himself once more on his bench, but this time not to work, but to rest.

"Nothin' more to tell, my dear. 'Ere I am, and folks can find me when they wants a job done."

"Don't you ever go away?"

"Only to do a job. This is my place. 'Oly Writ says: 'Trust in God and stay in thy place.' And this is my place, you see."

"How did you know it was?"

"I could feel A'mighty God needin' me here," said Barnabas. "That's vo-cation. Mebbe you think vo-cations are like jelly-moulds, jest a few stock patterns, Franciscan, priest, this kind-er nun and that. No. There's many of the same sort when it comes to monks and nuns, because A'mighty God can do with a big stock of them. But there's others 'E only wants one of for an odd job. Sin's made terrible 'oles in 'Is Plan, and 'E 'as to fill up those 'oles with queer characters that'll jest sarve to fit in, if you understand me?"

Philippa nodded.

"When you come to think of it," resumed Mr. Job, caressing Pansy, "it's a great privilege to serve an immartel soul. And even ... chapel-keepers have immartel souls; only, pore things, they got it smothered under their best weskits through allus wearin' Sunday clothes weekdays. Now I wears me weekdays Sundays, only cleaner, clean on Saturday in honour of Mary Immaculate, and 'oly confession. Now, let me give yer a cup more tea."

He poured out another cup skilfully.

"You'd be surprised 'ow many people thinks it beneath their dignity to 'ave an immartel soul," he mused. "But yer can allus find it, if yer looks for it."

"How do you find it?" asked Philippa, now vastly entertained.

"Same as I finds white vi'lets," said Mr. Job. "I goes to likely places. Look at things their ways, and feel things 'ow they takes them. That's the trick. Now, there was the new Squire's lady. A fiddle-faddlin' woman as ever I seed. 'Ighty-tighty and fidgetin' and whinin' about a job I was a day late with along of lumbago. Then the Squire goes sudden. The hinfloohenzia. And after that we never 'eard the last of 'im, with memorials and one thing and another. And she never came down to 'ave me dose 'er lap-dog, but it was 'Sir Thomas this' and 'Sir Thomas that,' what 'e would wish and what 'e never would 'ave permitted. But, yer see, that was where her immartel soul was, if you rummaged for it. It was no good trying to stop her or turn her mind. It don't do no good to poke a body any more 'n a parrot. I allus used to get her to think she was bein' kind and gracious to the pore, like as 'e'd have wished. I got 'er to come down with a little basket on 'er arm, with a pudden in it, feelin' gracious and nice, so she didn't remember to whine and be 'ighty-tighty. I never could bide pudden, but Pansy got proper fat on 'em, bad lad. All ladies oughter be gracious fer their own comfort. Besides," he added, and his voice lost its briskness and became almost dreamy, "I felt real sorry for her. She's 'ad all the sweet'earting she'll ever 'ave, pore soul. She'll never again hear the Squire say a love-name, silly like, as I s'pose 'e did when they were courtin'. She's got stiff and tall like that rose bush there that don't flower now."

He mused. Philippa did not feel inclined to break the silence. Then he looked up, and pulling off his glasses, which he had just discovered were still on his nose, he said:

"Now, you wouldn't think as I'd a sweet'eart, would you? I 'ave so. Dead this forty year. That's why I sets my affections on the things that are above, because they're along of my Jessie, and I allus did like to have my bits of savings all together. I reckon you're somebody's sweet'eart, my dear?"

"Yes," said Philippa.

"Ah," said Mr. Job. "And so that'll be your job, and well I reckon yer'll suit it. It's a tarrible lonely world for a man if he hasn't a sweet'eart to tell his troubles to. You'd be surprised. A dog's a good friend and so's a pipe, but when the evenings are long, I get thinking of my sweet'eart. I never did set much store by relations, along of me good mother's dying and the rester them mostly 'aving the same complaint. Weak wrist," he said with an indescribable gesture of drinking. "Couldn't stop pourin' it out. Only one of 'em left and she may be dead fer all I knows, pore gel—my sister Becky—as came to no good. My attic's ready fer 'er if my prayers git at 'er. But it's a sweet'eart we needs. I'm sorry for a man as 'asn't even got a sweet'eart in the life to come. And, if it comes to that, I never yet took to a woman's face as 'ad no sweet'eartin' lines in it, if you understand me. Lines with tryin' not to laugh tellin' 'im not to carry on so, and lines with wonderin' what 'ad 'appened when he was late. Sweet'eartin' sorrows," said Mr. Job, patting Pansy's head, "they're a two-edged sword, and sweet'eartin' joys are the honey of the world."

Philippa could not speak for a lump in her throat. She rolled her gloves in a ball and threw them for Pansy to fetch, and when he came back, wagging his whole body, eager for the approval he knew he would receive, she caught his velvet muzzle in her hands.

"Pansy," she said, "I must go. I have to go and see my sweetheart."

"There now," said Barnabas Job, interested at the hint of romance. "Pansy's got a sweet'eart—up at the Crown and Anchor, the bad lad."

Philippa laid a shilling on the table, and, picking up her walking-stick, held out her hand.

"Good-bye, Mr. Job," she said. "You have sent me on my way rejoicing. I shall come and see you again, but it won't be just yet, as I am going to be married."

"Bring your good gentleman," said Odd Job.

"I can't," she said gently. "You see, he is blind and a complete cripple. He was nearly blown to pieces in the war."

"My!" said Odd Job, very respectfully. "Now, that's a vocation Father Boneyvencher would just like to see. An odd job of

sweet'eartin'. Father Boneyvencher, of course never needed anyone, God A'mighty being 'is sweet'eart, in a manner of speaking,
but 'e would have liked a vo-cation like that. No, not a shilling,
missy. Only fourpence, and I wouldn't take that, but I owe it to St.
Anthony, which was a promise along of 'is finding the screw of my
mangle Toosday. The tea was . . ."

"An odd job?" asked Philippa, laughing. Her voice was not
quite steady, but Barnabas Job thought she looked radiant. The
tea certainly had revived her.

"More of a Feast," said Barnabas Job. "A little Feast 'll often do
as much good as a long fast to my immartel soul. Do you know
your way, missy?"

"Clearly," said Philippa. "Thank you for showing me." With a
wave of her hand, she was gone, walking swiftly and surely down
the road.

"Now, that's funny," said Odd Job to Pansy. "Bless me if I remembers showing her the way!"

The Chinker

"Not for me the vaunt of woe.
  Was I not, from a boy,
Vowed with helmet and spear and spur
  To the blood-red banner of joy?"

G. K. CHESTERTON

The Chinker

ARNABAS JOB picked himself up very slowly and painfully, and held his breath lest there should escape him one of the comments that, in the days of Alfred Jenkins, he had been accustomed to make only too fluently. The cocker-spaniel, collarless and unregenerate, wagged his stern appreciatively, and slobbered with mirth. Barnabas Job would not trust himself to look at the dog for a moment or two, but gave his attention to the end of his spine, which was possibly pulverised, and the seat of his trousers, which were probably done for. But no, thanks to a stout patch of Mr. Job's own sewing, the trousers were intact.

"Pansy," said Mr. Job at last, "Run agin them steps when I'm on 'em once more, and it's not an apostle you'll be, but the angel of death and an act of God. And me being in good dispositions and resigned ain't a-going to 'inder me giving you a leathering you'll not forget, yer slithery little . . ."

Pansy, believing with St. Thomas Aquinas that prudence is the queen of virtues, flung himself neatly flat, and with one wriggle was under the hedge and had gained the safety of the road, up which he ambled complacently for a quarter of a mile, without so much as stopping to inquire into any of the smells of rabbit and rat that came to him from the hedges. He knew the tone of voice that indicated his master's immediate intention to take off his leather belt and apply it to his loose-fitting skin, and although, dog-like, Pansy loved him the better for it, an opportunity to avoid the operation was not to be lost. So he would make his way to

101

the quarry for a real good serious rabbiting—much better sport than any hedge could provide. But luck was against Pansy that evening. Turning himself into a black frog for the second time in ten minutes, so as to get through the broken fence into the quarry, he emerged into the very lap of a man clad in tweeds, who was sitting on the grass there.

The man's voice said:

"H'm, a pedigree cocker."

There was nothing for it but to waggle ingratiatingly.

The editor of *The London Lanthorn* (who as all the literary, theatrical and social world knows, is Esmond Dentoun) found it difficult to criticise Pansy unbiassed by that waggle.

"Rather a nice little feller, bejabbers," he said, with a smile curving and beautifying his ugly mouth. "So you waggle, do you? And if I were a neat little spaniel, with a neat little starn and a gentle little jowl, I'm blest if I'd waggle to anybody—not to the King himself. Not," he said lazily, pulling Pansy's ears as though he had known him all his life, "if it were to a tobacco millionaire or the owner of the Sunday Press. Not to the Archangel Gabriel or Carnera. Not to the very devil himself."

Pansy wriggled himself free, stood back a step, and barked. Then he backed another step, barked again, and looked at Dentoun with his head on one side.

"Hullo," said Dentoun. "Want me to follow you, do you?" This interested him. He scrambled to his feet. Pansy slid through the hedge, and whined softly, excited. Dentoun put a long leg over the low hedge, and vaulted into the road. Pansy, who had forgotten all about the belting that his master had promised him, ran a little way down the road, and then back to Dentoun, running round him to express his appreciation of this strange man's intelligence in understanding and following.

"Well, dang my buttons," said Dentoun, "and dash my wig and weskit, where the doose is the faithful hound taking me to? I trust it is not a child with golden curls who has been run over by the re-vengeful—the r-revengeful Jasper, because, hound, the least little spot of gore and I shall come all over queer. What is it, you rum little start? All right, I'm a-coming like Christmas. Can't I even stop to do my bootlace up?"

Pansy, satisfied that Dentoun was following him in good ear-nest, proceeded ahead like a little steam-tug who was pulling the larger craft by an invisible hawser. And so they came, through the back gate, into Mr. Job's garden.

Barnabas Job, placidly at work on his pair of steps, heard Pansy's bark of greeting, and clutched frenziedly at the wall. But it was not necessary. Pansy did not bombard the steps. He sat down with his tongue out, laughing heartily at his success. Barnabas Job, glancing down, met the bewildered countenance of Esmond Dentoun.

"Afternoon, sir," said Barnabas, cheerfully.

"Good afternoon," returned Dentoun. "Can you explain why your dog fetched me here? I was sitting quietly down there by the quarries, and he appeared, and with every sign a dog could make, implored me to follow him. So I did."

"Trying to redeem 'is character, was 'e?" nodded Barnabas. "Yer bad lad. Cunning as a 'uman, 'e is, sir," he added, descending gingerly from the steps, and coming across the grass patch to his visitor. "Along of a circus he was, sir. Trained to fetch people to the sideshows of a fair. Broke 'is leg, and broke it bad, and they were for shooting 'im, but I got them to leave him with me. And then 'e got converted, and turned apostle, didn't yer, Pansy? Dog-pup," added Mr. Job, "but I calls 'im Pansy along of 'is face. Jest like the black part of a pansy. Yes, 'e got converted and turned apostle, and now 'e goes out into the 'ighways and the 'edges, and compels them to come in. I've known Pansy bite a tramp in the slack of 'is trousers to get 'im along for the sake of 'is immartel soul."

"Begorrah!" was all the critic of *The London Lanthorn* could find to say.

"'E'll pick on one and let the others go their own ways, same as the Lord," said Mr. Job, "and then, coaxing or frightening of 'em 'e'll get them 'ome.

"And then," said Barnabas Job, "sometimes the Lord gives me a word for them, and 'agin 'E don't. And if 'E don't, I gives them a cup-er tea, or mebbe a nice ripe Victoria, and minds them they didn't make theirselves nor yet keep theirselves going, and that God A'mighty must set tarrible store by them to do it, and, make a mock or not, you can't resist that it's a comfortable thought that God A'mighty's settin' store by the likes of you. And they don't put it out of their minds so quick as they purtends. Now which'll you 'ave, cup-er tea or a nice ripe Victoria?"

"I'm obliged to you," said Dentoun, who was never discourteous even when he was most cynical. "I should prefer a plum."

"Come round and choose four or five," said Barnabas heartily, approving of Pansy's choice from among the unregenerate. "I've a fine tree and a fine view from the front of me cottage. You see? Over Blackcombe village. Right back north to the Purley Gap— twenty, thirty miles. And right back south to the Pearly Gates!" He looked for Dentoun to smile and finding his joke appreciated, chuckled. "Right back south to the Downs, anyway," he said. "There now, try that, sir."

"But look here," said Dentoun, accepting the proffered plums, "what's all this about conversion? How do you begin? I am well aware I require conversion as much as anyone, but I don't see how you're going to begin. If I did, I am sure I'd help you. What admirable plums."

"That's a Victoria," said Barnabas. "I tried planting a young daily Prolific, but it didn't do as good. I'm all for progress, so long as the fruit's as good as the old kinds. But by their fruits ye shall know 'em. No, I don't know how I'm a-going to convart you, but the Lord does, or He'd never have wasted my time sending you along. The Lord's reasonable, though from the rubbish you 'ear talked in the newspapers, anyone 'ud fancy there was a loopy idiot or someone as you could stuff with a lot of talk rulin' the universe. There's no nonsense about the Lord, and that makes my 'eart go out to 'Im. You'd never find the Lord sending along some batty creetur as was unconvartible when I'm in the middle of me chinkin', and the putty gettin' fribble every minute."

"Chinkin'?" queried Dentoun, one eyebrow going up as it did when he did not understand.

"Canadian word," said Mr. Job, a thought consciously, as one who was something of a philologist. "Ever bin to Canada? I was there a matter of twenty years ago. Come the winter, a chap got a living going round the farms and chinkin' up any 'oles where the wind or the wet could come through. You needed a bit of money put by for a new roof or a new job of plastering, but you could get chinked up snug enough for very little. Now this bit of a place," he jerked his thumb at the cottage, "is thick enough in the walls, and the floors good enough, because I relaid them myself, and the roof's as thick as a 'aystack, but once the summer's gone for good, you'd be surprised the places the wind and the wet finds out. So I gets out a ladder, and a bit of moss and a bit o' putty, and there I'll be, snug as a woodchuck. Ever seen a woodchuck? American animile."

"Do you act as a chinker to the village?" Dentoun asked.

"That and any odd jobs," said Barnabas. "That's my vo-cation. Odd jobs. Chinkin' up their thatches and their souls, pore creeturs. You see, that's what odd chaps like me were made for, to shove into some 'ole to keep the east wind out, because there's sperritual east winds, if you take me, that'll ketch a 'uman being midribs and chill 'im down miserable and get 'im fretting with fever about the future, until 'e's stiff as a corpse with despair. I didn't choose to be created, but Pruvidance took and created me when there was an odd job or two for me."

"You're quoting Epictetus," said Dentoun. "'Thou didst not choose thine own time to come into existence,' he says, 'but came when the universe had need of thee.'"

"Eppy Teetus?" said Mr. Job, deeply interested. "I see eye to eye with 'im there. Is the gentleman livin'? No? Gone to 'is reward. Ah, well, it's very true. Would you mind if I fetched me lump o' putty and worked it, because if I leave it in this wind and sun, it'll be gettin' fribble?"

"Putty," said Dentoun, reminiscently, "I haven't handled putty since I was fifteen or so. I'll work it for you."

"That you shall and welcome," said Mr. Job. "Mebbe you'd like to see the bit of the roof I'm on to mendin'? I'll shut Pansy in the back-kitchen so 'e don't run agin the ladder and have us down, the scoundrel. In you go, Pansy, me lad. And now, sir, up and set on that sack I've put across the eave, and you'll have a good 'old."

Poised quite comfortably between heaven and earth, working the putty in his well-kept fingers, with the breeze stirring his hair and the sun warm on the back of his neck, Esmond Dentoun seemed to himself to be not in any extraordinary position, but as though he was back in his childhood with all its objective realities and placid sanities. Mr. Job's red-brown wrinkles reminded him of the coachman who had taught him to ride, and Mr. Job's gnarled hands, stowing the moss away in the treacherous place under the thatch, and reaching up to him now and then for a piece of the well-worked putty, seemed to be stopping chinks in his own life where not an east wind, but a cold strange breeze blew idly through his thoughts, lowering the temperature of his enthusiasms and sometimes making him shiver in his inmost soul.

"Chinking," he said dreamily. "A very old-fashioned trade."

"Ah," said Barnabas, "and no great demand for it nowadays. Folks reckon theirselves too fine. They goes for one of them dirty plumbers."

"Very true," said Esmond Dentoun. "We're not too fine to have one of them dirty plumbers in our house. That skunk Ranowski, for instance, with his infernal psycho-analysing of despair. A dirty plumber. Making such a mess in the intellectual bathroom."

Mr. Job had been unable to follow this.

"Oh, ar," he said dimly. "You don't get much call for chinking. Mebbe it's a good thing you don't, for there's no supply either."

"True," said Dentoun, his thoughts a thousand miles away with hatred of Ranowski. He would write an essay about Ranowski. It would make London sit up. An absolutely fresh point of attack.

"A wee bit more for here, if you please, sir," said Mr. Job, peering at his handiwork. "And that'll do for 'ere. Were you thinking of takin' up chinkin'?"

"Eh? Oh, here you are. Chinkin'? I? Well . . . I see." Astride the gable of the cottage, he could see the miles of meadow, forest and downland, with villages in between lying Londonwards. He imagined his own editorial office, and the make-up for the next number which would be lying on his desk. The rough rags of Rupert Nazesmith's verse, the bloodless conceits of P.J.K., the long brilliant essay about what was the matter with somebody else's essays. Destructive criticism and the praise of destructive critics. Only fantasy ever soared from his magazine, all the deep delving was plumbing by some dirty plumber, plumbing without adequate tools among the drains of existence, a business that seemed based on an agreement with some trade union never to set about it deftly and be done with it, never to come to an end of poking about in the mess of decay at the bottom of abnormal minds. No, there was no chinker on his staff. Nazesmith, P.J.K., Elliot-Brown, Lady Walner, none of them believed that life had any thatch worth mending. They were always poking holes in anything that sheltered anybody from any east wind of life. And yet, somehow, the right kind of wind never seemed to blow through, as it was blowing through his hair now. Only breezes that smelt like a laboratory, like the library of a collector of first editions. A London Lanthorn! Gas! Flaring, whistling, bluish, leaking, stinking gas!

"Are you comin' down, sir?" Barnabas Job repeated.

Dentoun's lean ugly face was chin-tilted towards the evening sky, and when Mr. Job spoke again it looked sideways at him absent-mindedly. Then consciousness stirred.

"Oh, yes. Done? Right. Wonderful view you have here. I must be going. Left my car at the golf-house a mile or two from here. Got to run back to town for dinner."

Still absentminded, Dentoun thrust the putty into his handkerchief, came down the ladder, shook hands sincerely with Mr. Job, patted Pansy, and strode up the road without really recovering full consciousness. He drove back to town in the same state and ran over a hen and the trilby hat of an infuriated pedestrian without being aware of either.

He had changed in the golf-house and he dined at Lady Walner's. His dinner-partner, who was a charming member of the Russian Ballet, shrugged her bare shoulder at him early on in the proceedings, and asked the man on her other side whether the adequate Dentoun person was often taken bleak like this. But Dentoun saved his reputation for being "interesting" when, taking out his handkerchief, he bewilderedly abstracted from it a large lump of putty. Laying this on his plate, he gazed at it, and was heard to exclaim to himself:

"Putty! And the feller never converted me after all!"

Maybe it was telepathy, for somewhere about that time, Mr. Job, searching in vain through his toolbag for the remains of the putty, remarked to Pansy who was sniffing round the tool shed for rats:

"Well, I don't understand the Lord, I'm sure. I took to that young man, but I'm 'bliged to believe 'e went off with me putty, and that before I'd time to do a thing to convart 'im."

The Deep Heart

"I sought only for the Heart of God, therein to hide myself"—JACOB BOEHME.

The Deep Heart

HROUGH THE WILD rose hedge the notice stuck out: "ODD JOB'S." And from behind the hedge, across a small garden in which vegetables and flowers grew amicably together, there came the sound of a cobbler's hammer.

Barnabas Job was mending a shoe that you would have thought quite past mending, and what's more, he was mending it at a great rate, working against time. When it was done, he would send in the bill—a bill that Rockefeller couldn't have settled—but that Timmy Brown could—"Pleas make your ferst Fryday kermunon for Mrs. O'Kell's elbert." Spelling, Mr. Job would have told you, wasn't his business. Mending a motherless child's shoes *was*. So was getting prayers for everybody's intentions.

He was working there, in his stone-flagged workshop that had once been a mere back-kitchen, half whistling and half humming a tune, when his elbow was jogged, and looking down over his spectacles he met the melancholy eyes and deplorable visage of the black spaniel.

"Git off, Pansy," he said. "Yer a bad lad. Might've 'ad that tack into me thumb."

But to his surprise, the nudge was repeated.

"'Ere!" said Mr. Job. "Didn't yer 'ear me, Pansy? What's the matter? What's the matter with yer?"

Pansy moved in the direction of the door, turned, fixed Mr. Job with his melancholy eye, came back a step or two as though to fetch him, and then moved back to the door.

"Oh dear," said Mr. Job, laying down the hammer and taking some tacks out of his mouth. "Whatever is it now? Last time I b'lieved you, yer bad lad, it was only a rabbit."

Pansy ignored Mr. Job's lack of faith, and led him briskly through the orchard and into the lane beyond, to where, sitting on a stile with her back to them, leaning against the oak-tree which formed one of the props of the stile, was a badly dressed middle-aged woman, staring ahead of her and twisting a handkerchief in her hands.

"There," Pansy seemed to say with his whole black satin body, "is that a rabbit or is it a case for you?"

"Arternoon, ma'am," said Barnabas Job cheerfully. "So Pansy here was right. You wasn't a rabbit."

The woman had started when he spoke, and had faced him with resentment, but nobody could look at that odd square-set figure with the grey hair smooth-parted, grey eyes wide-apart and snub nose, and continue to feel resentment.

"What do you mean?" she said sharply. "Not a rabbit? What ..."

"Well, you see," said Barnabas Job, "if Pansy comes and tells me as I'm wanted, mebbe it's a rabbit 'e's caught, and mebbe it's a body in a bit of trouble."

The woman stared at him.

"Do you mean to say your dog went and fetched you and brought you to me? I never heard of such a thing."

"Mebbe not," said Mr. Job. "But that's Pansy's vo-cation, like. Dog-pup, but I calls 'im Pansy along of 'is face. Jest like the black part of a pansy," he said, as he always did. "Pansy got converted and now 'e goes out into the 'ighways and the 'edges and compels them to come in."

"Come in?" said the woman, catching at the first word of which she could make sense. "Come in where?"

"Why," said Mr. Job, "into my kitchen for a cup-er tea. I'd be pleased if you would, ma'am. Don't do no good settin' alone

112

outside at tea-time. And there's a powerful lot of musqeeters 'anging about," he added.

The woman got down from the stile.

"You may be mad," she said wearily, "but I'm sure I don't care. I'd give anything for a cup of tea."

Drooping and bewildered, she followed the jaunty spaniel who led the way with the air of a victor bringing home the spoil. Beside her, Mr. Job talked placidly about the respective merits of the sevenpenny and the eightpenny quarter-packets of tea, and found his visitor in complete agreement with him as to the wisdom of paying the extra penny.

Once in the kitchen, he begged her to be so good as to make the tea herself to her own liking, and returning to his work on Timmy Brown's shoe, watched her at the soothing occupation of making tea and cutting bread and butter. When she had made the tea, he washed his hands, and taking his place at the table, said his grace. The woman made no comment, but eyed him curiously. But it was only when two cups of the admirable eightpenny brew had put some colour into her cheeks, and she had given Pansy a reluctant smile and a crust, that Mr. Job said:

"First Friday termorrer."

"What's that?" asked the woman. She had told him her name was Mrs. Kent.

Barnabas Job explained. It was the day dedicated to the Sacred Heart of Our Lord.

"I wasn't brought up to hold with any of that," said Mrs. Kent. "Read your Bible and be kind to others—that was good enough for us. But there's no religion nowadays. People are as hard as flints. You might die as you stood, for all they'd trouble. And yet if you ARE religious, what do you get out of it? I'm sure I've always done my duty and gone to church every Sunday evening ever since I was a girl, and what of it? My husband left me with a baby not four months old, and then the baby died. That was ten years ago, and

I've been working to support myself ever since. Had a good job as a housekeeper. And now the gentleman's married, and out I've got to go, and nobody cares whether I get another job or I don't. That's what gets me. They don't *care*. Full of their own selves, all the time."

"You're right," said Mr. Job, who knew the wisdom of agreeing with everything a woman said. "But would you blame me if I couldn't get the sea into a saucer?"

Mrs. Kent stared at him with distinct alarm. Oh, the man MUST be mad. He had picked up the bread-knife in a dreamy way.

"No. No, of course not," she said hurriedly. "Of course I shouldn't."

"Of course you wouldn't," said Mr. Job, cutting himself a slice of bread. "Well, the sorrers of the world are as deep as the sea, and the 'eart of man is as small as a saucer. We're full up with our own sorrers, and those of them as is nearest to us. Why, you couldn't get the sorrers of this village into your 'eart, ma'am. And what's this village compared to Lunnon? And what's Lunnon compared to Eu-rope and the world? 'Tain't possible. You might sorrer with ten, and yer might sorrer with twenty, but there'd come a time when you'd say: 'Oh, go away, I can't bear any more. I don't want to listen to any more.' You see, ma'am, you'd 'ave to be God A'mighty to take it all in and not die."

"You're right," said the woman. "It doesn't bear thinking of. It breaks your heart. Talk about God—you'd think that if there's a God it 'ud break *His*."

"That's jest what it did," said Barnabas Job. "God became man fer to get a 'uman 'eart to feel all like we feels and to hold it all and not to die of it, along of being God as well. The Sacred 'Eart. Don't yer read the Psalms? 'Man shall come to a deep 'eart.' Deep enough to take in everybody's sorrer. But yer can't expect nobody else to do it. They 'aven't room. Only if you're an apostle of the Lord, 'E enlarges yer 'eart, and you gets more like 'Im, and you can take in more. Look at Pansy. Never used to care for nowt but rabbits and the like. And now look at 'im gazin' up at yer, ever so sorry."

What woman could have prevented herself glancing down? And what woman, meeting those liquid eyes full of melancholy sympathy, could have stayed her hand from fondling his ears?

"He's a dear little dog, certainly," she admitted, not too grudgingly. "And I see what you mean. Of course there's a lot of trouble, and you can't expect to be considered as though you were the only one."

"Except by the Lord," said Mr. Job. "The Lord's got a wonderful way with 'Im of thinking each of us is the only one. You can take yer sorrer to the Sacred 'Eart as though it were the only sorrer in the world. And the Lord'll make you feel as 'E's thinkin' of nothing else. But 'E'll get *you* to think of something else. That's 'Is way. When my sweet'eart died, I couldn't think of nothink else but me own sorrer till I took it to the Sacred 'Eart, and then I found I kinder left it with 'Im and began to do a bit for other people's sorrers."

"Well, I'm sure I wish I could get like that," said Mrs. Kent.

"You wait till I've given that shoe a bit of a shine round," said Mr. Job, "and I rackon you shall. Fust cottage past that stile where you was sittin' is Brown's. Dirty old man. Got such a nice lil grandson. Timmy they calls 'im. Brown did ought to buy 'im some noo shoes, but it all goes on snuff and beer. But I've mended up 'is old ones grand, and ef you'd be so good as to take them along when you goes, mebbe you could tell the child what to do for 'is tuthache. Suffers with the tuthache, 'e does."

"Poor little thing," said Mrs. Kent. "Wants a bit of washing soda in it. I used to suffer that way myself as a child."

She watched Mr. Job, who had returned to his work.

"I've the offer of a job in these parts," she volunteered. "Not much, but you can't choose. Reckon I may as well accept it."

"Ar," said Mr. Job. "Do so. Mebbe you might keep an eye on Timmy Brown if you was round about. Rackon 'is sorrers wouldn't take up much room in anybody's 'eart, but 'e'd think 'isself in 'eaven if 'e got a bit er mothering and an interest took in 'is tuthache."

In his own mind, Mr. Job had decided that he would alter his message to Timmy. Mrs. O'Kell's Albert must wait till Sunday.

"If you'd take these along," he said, "tell Timmy from me that we'll call the bill settled if he'd offer his Communion termorrer for a lady as is very sad. And no need to tell him as I means yourself, ma'am."

Mrs. Kent took the shoes.

"I'm sure I thank you for the tea," she said. "I'm sure I do feel better. As for the little boy's offering . . . what you said . . . if it's any kind of praying, he better pray for his toothache. It's bad for a child to have pain. At my age, we ought to be able to bear it. Good evening, and thank you. I'm sure I hope we shall meet again."

Barnabas Job looked after her.

"Rackon the Lord did that without any pertickler prayin'," he said. "Mebbe 'E knew as I'd settle up with 'Im termorrer, and did it on credit, like."

Love-Lies-Bleeding

"Now there was in the place where he was crucified, a garden."—ST. JOHN xix, 41.

Love-Lies-Bleeding

"EXCUSE ME," said the young man in grey, "but could you sell us some flowers?"

Barnabas Job straightened himself and regarded the speaker. There was a beautiful blue touring car in the lane, and behind the man a woman whose shining hair showed under a little hat which even Mr. Job realised was a very special kind of hat— the kind of hat that doesn't happen every day. It looked like a kind of a crown, only put on crooked, as though you were too happy to wear it straight.

"Well," said Mr. Job, returning to the question of flowers, "mebbe I could. How many would you be wanting?"

"As many as this lady can hold in both hands," said the man.

Mr. Job glanced at the lady, and her ripple of laughter and his deep chuckle sounded together.

"So that's the way you want them," said Mr. Job. "Rackon I could. Would you be pleased to come in, ma'am?"

He laid down his rake, and opened the gate for her. Down the path, like a cannon-ball, came Mr. Job's black spaniel. But the lady fielded him neatly, and fondled him.

"Oh, do look, Pierce! What a darling!"

"Do you want him too?" said the man, looking at her as though she must have a dozen spaniels if she wanted them, and the moon and the stars as well if they pleased her.

She blushed.

"How could we take a spaniel?"

119

"Nothing is impossible . . . now," said the man in a low voice.

Now why, wondered Mr. Job, should she sigh when he said that, and turn away and finger the lemon-verbena as though she wanted to talk of something else?

"Would you like a bit of that to begin with?" he asked her, producing a clasp-knife out of his pocket. "And a bit of Lad's Love?"

The young man laughed.

"Oh yes, we must have a bit of Lad's Love," he said. "Mustn't we, Viola? And what's this blue thing? Let's have some of that."

"Anchusa," said Mr. Job, stooping over it. "But it droops if you cut it, it do. Looks as sad as a 'uman. Now take some of them c'nations. Fine for lasting. And a bit of blue rosemary. Rosemary for remembrance."

"No, we don't want any of that," said the young man. "My . . . er . . . the lady doesn't care for it."

"Very good," said Mr. Job imperturbably.

"Oh, what's this funny thing?" asked the lady called Viola, rather as though she wanted to talk of something else.

"Ah," said Mr. Job, "that's what we calls 'Love-Lies-Bleeding.' It's an old name."

"I wonder how they thought of it," mused the lady named Viola. "Love-Lies-Bleeding . . . of course it is the colour of blood, but those long ropes of flower . . ."

"Rackon it put them in mind of the Scourging of Our Lord," said Barnabas Job.

The south wind sighed among the flowers in the silence that hung heavy after his words. The young man turned away, and examined a stonecrop, but the lady stood poised in stillness, her eyes suddenly dark with the portent of those words. Love . . . lying bleeding. The country people, so wise, had not called Him "Lord"; they had called Him "Love." The afternoon heat shimmered over the garden. In the meadow beyond a lark hung in the sky, twittering his golden music. The elms were almost black with their July foliage. Down in the lane the touring car waited. ". . . the Scourging of Our Lord."

"Canterbury bells?" suggested Mr. Job. "Round these parts they calls 'em 'Cups-and-Sarcers' but I likes the old name meself. Rackon it's so old as the days when they went on pilgrimage to Canterbury and heard a fine peal of bells ringin' out to welcome them."

"I never thought of that," said the young man. "Did you, Viola?"

"Never," she said, and her tone was still very pensive.

"Talkin' about cups and sarcers," said Barnabas Job. "Mebbe the lady and you would like a cup er-tea, sir? Kittle's a-bilin'. A nice cup er-tea and some bread and butter and watercress?"

The young man glanced at the lady named Viola, but she had already nodded at Mr. Job.

"How kind of you," she said. "I should like it so much."

So leaving Pansy to entertain his guests, Barnabas Job went into his back kitchen.

"Come on, Kittle," he said, "the Lord's sent yer a job. Bile quick, there's a good kittle. If yer asks me, 'tain't all as right as it should be a-t'ween them. So bile quick afore she changes 'er mind."

Most people will do their best if they are asked in the right way, and perhaps kettles are no exception to this rule. Anyhow, it certainly happened that tea was ready in record time. When Mr. Job went to announce its readiness to his guests, he found the young man talking very earnestly in a low tone, and the lady looking far away at the horizon, very pensively. When he approached, they turned quickly, and the lady followed him with a pretty speech of appreciation for his quickness.

"Be pleased to set down, ma'am. And you there, sir. Ah, you didn't ought to thank me for being quick. That belongs to Kittle. Rackon a kittle's very Christian. Always seems so pleased to be useful. Sings away there, settin' on the stove, and don't get nuthin' for himself. Only cold water."

"Oh dear," said the lady, "I think it must be a saint, then. Going on trying to be good and only thinks of others and gets nothing but cold water."

She spoke almost desperately, as though she had tried it.

"Ar well, ma'am," said Barnabas Job, "as you knows well, 'tis givin' that makes us happy. Rackon as Kittle don't want to be different. Hope your tea's to your likin'? Eightpence a quarter and worth the extra. The sevenpenny's poor stuff."

"It's beautiful," said the lady. "And so is the watercress. Have some, Pierce."

All the same, she didn't eat no more than a canary, thought Mr. Job.

After tea, they went back into the garden, and Mr. Job insisted on taking them to the side of the house where, on the south wall, there was the climbing red rose with its load of flower. His visitors agreed that they had never seen anything like it.

"Do many people want to buy flowers?" asked the lady.

"A good few," said Barnabas. "But I tells them that they can have what they chooses, but I don't take money for them. No, no, ma'am," as she protested. "You can't sell what costs you nuthin'. Pruvidance gives me them roses, and I rackon I didn't ought to sell 'em. Besides, as I say, you knows that it's givin' as makes us happy, and I did ought to thank you for acceptin' them."

"I never heard such a charming speech," said the lady called Viola earnestly. "Thank you very, very much. Please give me some, and I shall treasure them."

She signed to Pierce to put away the ten-shilling note he had ready in his hand.

"Ay, so I will," said Mr. Job, putting a short ladder into position. "Now don't git bouncin' agin me, Pansy," he said to the spaniel. "Which ones takes your fancy, ma'am?"

"That one," said the man, pointing. "A perfect one."

Barnabas Job stretched out his hand, but as the knife touched it, it fell, petal by petal, at their feet. The lady turned and caught the man's arm.

"Pierce," she said, in a whisper, "that was an omen. We mustn't take it."

"Darling, don't be superstitious."

"I'll cut you some buds, ma'am," said Barnabas. "Always in its glory jest this time of the year. Rackon it comes out for the feast of the Precious Blood." He turned on the ladder and pointed. "Curious, ain't it, how flowers seem to know about a feast? 'Tain't only the roses. 'Tis the Love-Lies-Bleeding, and them red daisies and over there, that field of trefoil. Father Boneyvencher says they calls it 'Holy Blood' in France. Jest lives till the Feast of St. Mary Magdalen."

He turned back, and went on cutting the crimson buds. Below, no movement or word broke the silence. Only the lark.

Then Mr. Job spoke.

"And now I'll git you jest one or two of my yaller roses. Glory roses, some calls 'em. But I calls 'em Butter-and-Honey."

"Butter-and-Honey," said the lady named Viola, to the man called Pierce. Mr. Job was up the ladder and they were alone below. "That is the last sign. You know. 'Butter and honey . . . that he may know the evil and choose the good.' Pierce, we can't. You can say what you like. We know it's wrong, wrong. And nothing could make it right. God has stopped us. And all this garden's full of . . . of the Precious Blood. We couldn't. I am going back to John, and however impossible he is, I'm going to try again. You must go back by train. Don't you see, it's like the angel with the flaming sword. We are Catholics, and it would mean refusing the Precious Blood."

"But you said you loved me," said the man, unable to say more.

"So I do. So much that I won't let you lose your soul for me. Pierce," breathlessly, "it will be terribly hard, but we shall have the grace . . . great grace." Tears stopped her. The man could only look at her, miserably.

123

Barnabas Job didn't seem to be surprised when the man didn't follow her into the car. He simply put the flowers in her lap. Then he said: "Bide a moment," and went back, to return with something in his hand. Her eyes were too blurred to see what it was.

"Mebbe you'd like a bit of Love-Lies-Bleeding after all," he said. "Kinder holy."

She took it with fingers that shook, and then turned to the man who stood in the road beside her.

"Oh, kiss it, Pierce," she said. And when he did so she put it back in her lap, pressed her foot on the starter and drove away before they could realise it.

The man stood looking after her and then—having forgotten Barnabas Job—he turned and walked away in the other direction.

Barnabas Job stood at the gate, pulling through his fingers the crimson rope of flowers—a broken spray that had been dropped.

"'Tain't always a thunderbolt and a flamin' sword," he said. "Rackon 'E's most wonderful when 'E's so gentle. Drove 'em back to 'Is grace with a lil scourge of flowers wot wouldn't 'ave 'urt a tom-tit. Rackon yer've got to be Love 'Isself to be so tarrible gentle."

And for a long time Barnabas leant on his gate with the crimson rope in his gnarled hands as though he were meditating on a relic.

Bank Holiday with Barnabas

"For a cap and bells our life we pay
  And wear ourselves out with toiling and tasking.
It is only God who is given away:
  It is only Heaven may be had for the asking."

LOWELL.

Bank Holiday with Barnabas

UGUST BANK HOLIDAY had dawned radiantly and had grown more brilliantly sunny and more intolerably hot every hour. Down the roads, usually so quiet and empty, there rushed streams of cars; and in the meadows, the grass was beaten down by trippers. The ordinary inhabitants of Blackcombe village kept indoors, except for those who set up a trestle table outside their cottages and sold eggs and milk and flowers to all comers.

But Barnabas Job did a roaring trade on Bank Holiday. Not with any of the commodities that the other cottagers sold. In fact, he didn't sell anything. But he put up a notice: "You are Welcome to a Cup of Cold Well Water Free." And those who came in, expecting to be pressed to buy something else, went away disappointed at not being allowed to buy so much as a rose.

At the back of his cottage, just outside his back kitchen, Mr. Job had one of the finest old wells in the county. And the surveyor had told him that it gave the best water for miles, fed as it was, underground, from Laughing Source up in the forest. On Bank Holiday he tidied away the tools of his trade from that back kitchen which he used as a workshop, and set out some deck-chairs of his own making in the shade of the lime trees near the well. And then he waited for those whom Providence would send him, and instead of repairing boots and shoes, he took a holiday and repaired tempers.

All day he coped with his visitors—tired women in their best shoes, dragging crimson-faced children and disgruntled men who

127

had had to spend money on train fares that they would have preferred to spend on beer. In Mr. Job's deck-chairs, under the cool of the limes, they sat, clasping thick glasses of well water, listening to the hum of his bees, and finally having a bit of a sleep. Some of the children would be lured into Mr. Job's back kitchen, and there, girded with a roller towel, he would wash their poor little feet, while they sat on a wooden chair and wondered at him. And quiet and good they would listen to one of his fairy tales, and finally help him to "fix" a pretty nosegay to take to Mother when she woke up. In the memory of a good many children there must have remained the picture of that haven of coolness and quiet. It must have given them some idea of heaven.

It was late in the afternoon—about tea-time, when his other guests had departed to have tea at one of the cottages that provided it—that Mr. Job, straightening chairs, heard steps on the flags, and looked up to see come into his garden a lady with a white lace parasol and a white lace scarf round her shoulders, and beside her a girl so like her that she could only be a daughter—in a dress of flowered muslin and a wide shady hat. They both wore long gloves, and people with long gloves did not often visit Barnabas Job on Bank Holiday.

"Good afternoon," said the lady, with a gracious inclination of her head. "May we come in and beg a glass of water?"

"We very nearly ran over a little boy in the road outside, and in avoiding him, the chauffeur damaged the car and gave us a bad shaking," explained the girl. "My mother has been badly startled."

"And welcome," said Mr. Job, with his best bow. "Now would your ladyship like a chair there under the limes? And Missy too? I'll be getting two clean glasses."

When he disappeared into his back kitchen, Lady Manvers and her daughter exchanged glances.

"Does he know me?" asked Lady Manvers, sinking thankfully into a chair. "Oh, Lilas, how delicious!"

"No, he doesn't know us. The 'ladyship' was a mere token of respect in general. I like being called 'Missy.' Here he comes."

Barnabas reappeared, polishing two immaculately shining glasses, to give the ladies confidence in their inviolate cleanliness. Then he began to turn the handle of the well.

Lilas Manvers felt she must see the bucket coming up. She went over to the well, and saw it creeping up, wonderfully far away. She looked up into the old tiled roof of the well, and the first thing that met her eye was a little plaque of cheap French make hanging from the nail.

"The Immaculate Heart of Mary," she breathed. "Why! Are you a Catholic? Oh, then, do pray for me. I want to be a nun, and my mother is trying to prevent me and I want her to go on this afternoon to see Mother Prioress at the Benedictine Abbey over at Great Dunstanes. I'd just got her to say she'd come, and now she's making an excuse of this accident to say she can't go any farther. Do pray."

"Very good," said Mr. Job, still working the creaking wheel. Confidences were never a surprise to him.

Up came the bucket, and the glasses were dipped in by Lilas, and carried over to Lady Manvers, who sipped it, exclaimed at the delicious coldness, and beckoned to Mr. Job.

"But this is very kind of you," she said when he came. "Why do you go to all this trouble? Why not charge—say, a penny a glass, just to recompense yourself for your time and trouble? Won't you sit down and talk to us? You must be tired."

"Your ladyship is very thoughtful," said Mr. Job, taking a wooden chair and looking up into the face on which selfishness was writ clear in the petulant lines round the eyes and mouth. He knew quite well that Lady Manvers was more anxious that she should be entertained than that he should be rested. He answered her question. "Because, if your ladyship had an endless tub o' money that never got any emptier, standin' outside yer house, yer ladyship 'ud be glad to see them as needed it helpin' theirselves. Pruvidance gives me a well o' water, and why shud I sell it, seein' as 'ow I don't make it?"

"What a nice way of looking at it," said Lady Manvers. "It is beautiful water—so refreshing."

"Ar," said Mr Job. "Purest water for miles, so they tell me. Now down in the next village, they have to be usin' charcoal filters. Gets their charcoal up in the forest beyant." He jerked his thumb. "Many's the job o' charcoal burnin' I've done. Very slow. Learns yer a powerful deal, charcoal do."

"What does it . . . I mean, what do you learn?" asked Miss Manvers.

"Why," said Barnabas, "rackon it learns you the secret of life."

Lady Manvers was all attention. This sounded occult. She had heard of old folk in villages who knew strange mysteries.

"Do tell us," she said, holding her parasol so that she could see his brown face with the wide-apart eyes.

"Why," he said, "'tis very simple. What's charcoal? A bit of green wood with the life burnt out of it. Dead burnt wood. Ar. But you take a bit of green wood and put it at the bottom of some water and leave it so. What'll it do? Rot, and turn the water stagnant and crawling. But you take a bit of charcoal and put it at the bottom of some water, and what'll it do? Purify it. Take all the 'arm out of it, and take no 'arm itself. Charcoal can't rot. For why? 'Cause it's dead already. So, in a way, it's immartel. Now that's true of men and wimmen. You take some of 'em. Put 'em where you will, they turns things bad. For why? 'Cause they're full o' their own life—selfish. Take others and put 'em in the middle of any circumstances, and they'll take all the 'arm out of them, sweeten 'em, bring out the best in anybody, 'elp everybody to do what's right. For why? 'Cause they're dead to themselves and immartel. That's the Resurrection. Now, Missy," he said, wheeling round to the surprised Lilas, "I've 'ad a 'ard day of it, fetchin' and carryin'. Then you comes along. And when I goes to the well for you, I sez a bit of a prayer to the 'Macculate 'Eart of Mary along of my 'aving 'er picture there and me bein' that tired-like. And . . ." (Lilas could not imagine what he was going to say. Was he going to betray her confidence?) "And then," he went on serenely, "what does 'er ladyship say, ever so kindly: 'Sit down,' she says. 'You must be tired,' and talks ever so encouraging. Now you young people, Missy, you don't know what a gracious word'll do sometimes."

Lady Manvers had made a laughing gesture to stop Mr. Job, but he would go on.

"Now, Missy, what are you going to be? Goin' to get married?"

Lilas realised that this was her cue.

"I hope I am going to be a nun," she said.

"Ar," he said, "I'm not surprised. It's the good mothers who have daughters with the grace of a vo-cation. Never think of theirselves, they don't. Jest think of your holy vo-cation. Ar. Would your ladyship excuse me? There's something as I'd like to fetch."

Fascinated, the woman watched him trot off to the well—unhook something, and bring it back. It was the poor little plaque. On his way back he stopped at the flower-bed, pulled out his clasp-knife, and cut three or four magnificent white roses. These, with the plaque, he brought and laid respectfully on Lady Manvers' lap.

"I'd like your ladyship to accept it," he said, "as a token of esteem. There ain't no onselfishness like giving up your daughter. 'Tis like the charcoal and Our Lady as gave up her Only Son and never thought of herself."

Lady Manvers' words of protest and the tears that started into her eyes were sincere. It was a very humble Lady Manvers who climbed into the mended car, with Mr. Job's gifts in her white hands.

"We are on our way to the Abbey now to see Mother Prioress," she told Mr. Job. "And but for the rest in your garden, I shouldn't have felt strong enough to go."

Lilas could only press the old man's horny hand and thank him mutely.

"'Tworn't 'umbug," said Barnabas Job to himself, as he watched the car out of sight. "'Twere faith. I asked Our Blessed Lady to change 'er 'eart, and then I acted as though it WERE changed. And rackon it were."

The Laughing Source

"Therefore the world her baby is,
    That like a hurt and frightened child
    Sobs on her breast, the Undefiled,
Or hides its face upon her knees."

KATHARINE TYNAN.

The Laughing Source

BOUT A MILE beyond Barnabas Job's cottage, where a flank of the Downs sloped down into forest, there was a place called Green Hill which, in September, was deep in bracken. And here Barnabas was wont to go, in the evenings, sometimes. He would come through the forest, and climb up the stony path among the bracken and heather—the heather rustling over his boots and the bracken waist-high on either side of the path that was only a sheep-track—until suddenly the humming silence would contain a sound other than the birds' songs—the sound of running water. And a turn of the path would bring him to the very brink of a tiny, swift-rushing stream that poured out of the very heart of the hill, bubbling up from a fern-edged grotto no bigger than a cradle, and falling down into a round pool that was said to be unfathomably deep.

Pansy, the black cocker-spaniel, would wade into the narrow brink and, standing there on the sloping rim of sand, quench his thirst with gusto after what he pretended was a very long walk. He had certainly made so many excursions to right and left after rabbits that he had probably walked seven times as far as his master, but a cocker-spaniel as young as Pansy has to pretend to be tired very often, to hide the fact that he doesn't know what tiredness is.

Mr. Job, on the other hand, was always tired by the time he arrived there, because it was a walk he only took at the end of a working day, and his legs were not as young as they had been. So he would sit down on a tree that had fallen conveniently to form a seat of just the right height, and pull out his pipe and puff away "jest to keep the musqueeters away."

Today, however, Mr. Job's pipe was already drawing well by the time he arrived, because the musqueeters had been tarrible tiresome in the forest—Mr. Job called all flies musqueeters—and so he just sank down on the tree with a sigh of content. Pansy, panting a great deal, came out of the undergrowth and made for the stream; but suddenly pulled up short, and listened, and then whined, and then scuffled himself under the bracken.

There was a sudden yell of alarm.

"'Ello! 'Ello!" said Mr. Job, taking out his pipe. "'Ello? Pansy? Come 'ere."

Now he could hear a child crying noisily, as though it had been frightened badly. And before he could do more than get to his feet, there was a clashing of bracken stems and a swishing of fronds, and there appeared a very small girl in a pinafore with frills on the shoulders and her hair tied up on one side with a crimson ribbon—long, fine, hazel-brown hair. The small nose was swollen with long weeping and so were her cheeks.

"Come along to Uncle Barny," said Mr. Job, who never knew how many nieces and nephews he had until he met a fresh one. "C'm' along. Pore lil gurl. That pup won't 'urt you, ducky."

She had reached the horny brown hands that were held out to her, and had put her own small scratched ones into them with unconscious obedience to the quintessential uncle in Mr. Job.

"What's the matter, eh? What's your name?"

"Dora. It's my . . . my birfday."

"Well I never," said Mr. Job, hoisting her on to his knee. "Your name's Dora and it's your birthday. Well, what are you doin' cryin' on your birthday?"

"Bup-pup-gug-gug."

"That ain't tellin' me nuthin'," said Mr. Job. "Now you tell Uncle Barny what's wrong and I'll make it better," he added omnipotently.

Dora sobbed for a while with the satisfaction of every child who had ever discovered the solid consolation of Mr. Job's tobacco-smelling corduroy waistcoat; and then, wriggling two fingers into the fob pocket like a flower taking root in the cranny of a southern wall, she came out with:

"D-don't want to have hatpins stuck in my heart!"

"Well, that's reasonable enough," said Mr. Job. "'Oo's proposin' to stick 'em in?"

"F-father O'Sullivan."

"Lord bless us!" A vision of mild, short-sighted Father O'Sullivan making a pincushion of Dora was more than Mr. Job could bear, and he laughed aloud in the most comforting way.

"But . . . but . . . that's why they named me Dora . . . and he gave me this . . . and I've got to be exactly like it."

With the incoherence of a child making a detailed explanation, Dora produced a large cheap medal. "Look!"

Mr. Job shut one eye and peered at it closely with the other.

"Why, you little stupid 'un! It's Our Lady of Sorrows!" Then he understood, and laughed longer than ever. (It would have taken more education than Mr. Job had undergone to connect "Dora" with the Feast of Our Lady of Sorrows. The fact was, she had been baptised "Dolores"—which the aunt who had adopted her when her parents died, soon turned into "Dora.")

"Now you listen to me," he said, gathering the child close and clasping one grubby little hand safe in his wide palm. "You've mistook Father O'Sullivan's meanin'. You ain't got to 'ave anything stuck into yer, duckie. You've missed 'is meanin'. And anyway, them's swords, not 'at-pins. And not real swords, but jest to put us in mind of the sorrers of Our Blessed Mother. But to my mind there's a better way of thinkin' of them. Would you rather be like this nice lil stream?"

"Y-yes, please." Dora felt he could alter her destiny at will.

"Now you consider this lil stream, duckie. It comes right out of the side of the 'ill, beautiful and clear, don't it?"

"Yes." (It was a consoled and interested little "yes" this time.)

"Well, that's like the life of Our Blessed Lady and it's like your life's got to be. Beautiful and clear. And it falls straight down into the well, don't it, very deep and silent. Well, that's like Our Lady before the Angel came to 'er. And that's like you've got to be in yer 'eart, so quiet that yer kin 'ear God speak."

Dora nodded.

"And if you look over beyant, down to the meadow, you'll see it's got to run over stones and rocks and all among the nettles and the thorns, an't it? Well, that's like Our Lady's life when she had to go to meet all 'er sorrers, and like we all 'as to do. But you mind this. What do they call it when it falls down into that big pool near the village? They calls it Weeping Well. Ar. But what do they call it up here? Laughing Source. Now you mind that. Your life comes out'n the 'Eart of God and that's why children laughs so much. And if you keeps near to God, you'll allus be full o' laughter, duckie. And if so be as you've a long way to go and all among stones, if you don't look at the stones but keep listenin', you'll 'ear your own 'eart still laughin' because you comes from God and are goin' to 'Im. See? And Weeping Well ain't the end of the journey. Weeping Well is what you give to them as needs what you can give. If there weren't Weeping Well, we'd all be thirsty in the village, and if we didn't get no water, we'd die. Well, unless you 'as a bit of sorrer you can't be no 'elp to others. Now you've 'ad a bit of a scare, you'll be sorry for other lil gurls as is scared, won't yer? An' you'll be kind to them, won't yer?"

Dora nodded against his waistcoat.

"And as I says, Weeping Well ain't never the end of the journey. Where do the stream go then? Into the sea, don't it? Into the great blue sea—as is like God, same as the 'ill is. That's where Our Lady's life went, and that's where yours will—back to God. Not afraid of God, are yer?"

"Oh, no."

"You wud be a grand little stupid if yer was. Now d'yer understand about Our Lady of Sorrers? As how she only 'ad some sorrer so as she'd understand to comfort us? And that her 'eart's full o' laughter because she's so near God and because she's made us all so 'appy by givin' us Our Lord?"

Another nod.

"Very good," said Mr. Job. "And now what d'you say to a bit of a paddle? Do a bit of meditatin' with our feet? It's too deep fer us up 'ere, but down among the stones we can manage it. You see, we might drown among 'er joys, but we're safe in 'er sorrers and you kin wash yer face, duckie. Ask Our Lady to wash yer tears away and make yer cool and clean, eh?"

How much Dora had comprehended was doubtful, but a child absorbs and stores what it cannot understand. A little while later, with her skirts kilted up as far as they would go, she stood listening.

"What can you 'ear?" asked Mr. Job.

"She's laughin'," said the very small girl whose tears had been washed away.

A Rose for October

St. Hildegarde, in a vision, saw Heaven in the form of a rose, the choirs of Angels and of the Blessed being like the petals round the golden heart—the Blessed Trinity.

A Rose for October

HE COTTAGE stood out white against the green hill-side that rose up behind it. And round the cottage, in October, were the splendours that people came from neighbouring villages to see. Roses. Red, yellow, pink and white. Heavy-petalled, stiff-petalled, ramblers and standards, bush-roses and climbing ones that covered the sunniest side of the cottage and tapped at Barnabas Job's bedroom window. Early roses and late autumn ones were the kinds he favoured. And by clever coaxing and pruning he managed to have two crops of them—one in June and one in October. Of course, there was the great crimson one that flowered in July, and the Gloire de Dijon that kept it company; but it was June and October to see the whole garden at its best.

When it was fine, Barnabas Job would bring his cobbling out of doors, and every child in the village developed an anxiety to run errands with anybody's shoes that required attention, because everybody who called on Barnabas then would go away with a rose. Lady Barton would come in more than once in those months to wonder why his varieties did so much better than hers. Her husband had been Squire, and she still felt that, in some way, the village belonged to her, and that it was slightly disrespectful of anybody's roses to be better than hers. But Barnabas would hobble jauntily round on his bow legs in their corduroy breeches, his thumbs in his waistcoat, pointing out with a nod the flower that demanded her attention, and frequently stretching out that long-fingered hand, brown and work-worn, to cut the finest bud for her.

"Why do you cut her the best ones?" asked young Mrs. Alastair Graeme (whom Barnabas Job had first known as Philippa Lovel). "She has such wonderful gardens of her own."

"Ar. Pore soul," said Mr. Job, "and gets no good of 'em. It's little 'appiness she gets out of anythink. Some folks ruins their di-gestion for 'appiness by stuffin' theirselves with pride and pleasure. But what's pride? Sperritual ginger-beer. Fills you full of gas. And what's pleasure? Like them cheap sweets the children buys—gives yer tuthache and spiles yer appetite and makes yer sickly. Spilt 'er appetite, she 'as. And now nothink'll give 'er 'arf a moment's pleasure but my best Laurette Messimy which I got the cutting from my cousin in Kent. But lil Timmy Brown, 'e'll come along with 'is granfer's boots which as it's not mendin' so much as a merrickle they needs, and ef I give 'im a bud of that old Glory, all crookit and spiled, you watch 'im sniff it and give a great sigh and off 'e goes shoutin' and jumpin'."

Philippa's eyes were tender. All the village knew that ragamuffin of a Timmy. Of late, he had grown stouter and cleaner, for a friend of Mr. Job's, Mrs. Kent, had come as working housekeeper to Major Fotheringay who lived at The Corner House, and she had become a kind of fairy godmother to Timmy, finding time to mend and wash his clothes, to scrub his brown neck, and to have him up to The Corner House and smuggle him into the kitchen for a square meal now and then—a proceeding Major Fotheringay may have known more about than he appeared to, for the Major's eyeglass pretended not to see a good deal, but there was a shrewd grey eye behind it.

"Now your good gentleman," said Mr. Job, taking out his clasp-knife which was rarely idle for an hour together, "if I were to cut 'im that rain-dashed old cabbage pink, 'ud get more jy out of it than Squire's lady would outer five acres."

Philippa's smile was dewy. Alastair had taken on a new lease of life since his marriage, but it could not give him back his sight (indeed, he could see nothing at all now), or move him out of that long wheeled carriage. Still, gone were the black moods that had been the most intolerable relic of his wounds and shell-shock. Alastair was very fond of coming to visit Mr. Job, especially when the roses were out. Job, with the perfect tact that doesn't try to pretend, would put a rose in the blind man's sensitive hands, and challenge him to guess the colour.

"'E's got that cunning of late," said Mr. Job, "that I wouldn't wager a bad sixpence on his not bein' able to guess a colour now. Rackon 'e kinder *feels* it."

He was cutting roses for Philippa when a voice over the hedge distracted him.

"Er . . . haw . . . er . . . just a moment."

Mr. Job and Philippa looked up. There stood Major Fotheringay, grey hat in hand and considerable embarrassment on his narrow critical face.

"Ah . . . How d'you do, Mrs. Graeme? There's some trouble here."

"Where?" Philippa could see nothing.

"Er . . . ah . . . Fact is, it's holding on to the leg of my . . . my trousers."

Sternly repressing the desire to laugh, Philippa ran down the path and out of the gate. Mr. Job followed.

There in the lane stood the Major, and holding on to the Major's elegant grey trouser was a very small girl weeping in despair.

"Lord luv yer, it's Rosie Binns," said Mr. Job, gently pushing Philippa aside. "Let me come, my dear. She don't care about wimmen, don't Rosie. Allus takes 'er troubles to me or Farmer Briggs, and now she's got the Major."

Stooping down, he detached the grubby fingers from the Major's trouser-leg, and picked up the small wriggling figure in his strong old arms.

"Narty gurl you are to ketch holt of the Major," he said, taking out his clean old red handkerchief to wipe her eyes. "And yer fingers all sticky. Where are yer 'urt, now?"

There then proceeded from Rosie a series of wails and sniffs and chokes and yells that indicated to Philippa and Mr. Job that Rosie had been unable to get her own way. The Major, considerably concerned, believed the child to be about to die of choking, having swallowed something hard.

"Send for the doctor," he said. "The child's in great pain."

"Not a bit of it," said Mr. Job. "That ain't stummick, that's temper. Hollering for pain's as different as hollerin' for temper as the cuckoo's different from a turkey. Now, Rosie! Stop it. Ef you don't stop it, the Major'll go away."

"No," blubbered Rosie.

"Yes 'e will. Now tell Uncle Barny wot yer was cryin' for."

More sniffs and sobs. But there finally emerged the fact:

"I wants to be in the miggle."

"Now . . ." said the Major, putting in his eyeglass. "What the dev . . . er . . . what the dickens is a miggle?"

But Mr. Job needed no explanations.

"Miggle of what, ducky?"

"T'resa an' Luthy an' Jamie an' Elthy."

"And where are Teresa and Lucy and Jamie and Elsie?"

"Runned away."

"Then you must a' bin pesterin' 'em," said Mr. Job. "Because Teresa's a good little sister to you. You must a' bin pesterin' them to let you be in the middle all the time."

"Yeth," acknowledged Miss Rosie, turning sulky eyes on the Major with a piteous appeal for sympathy.

"Well, you can't expect them always to let you be in the middle," said Mrs. Graeme.

Rosie turned her back on Mrs. Graeme.

"Now," said Mr. Job, "you let me wipe yer nose and yer eyes, and then I'll tell yer a story."

"Thtory?"

"Yes."

Rosie turned to the Major.

"Thit down for a thtory," she ordered, indicating a wheelbarrow in the hedge.

Fearful of provoking another outburst of tears if he demurred, the Major eased the knees of his grey trousers and sat down on the wheelbarrow, indicating the other side to Mrs. Graeme. And so, with a grin, Mr. Job had to accept an audience of three.

"Well," he said, "it's like this. One of these fine days, you and me, Major, and Mrs. Graeme, and Teresa and Lucy and Jamie and Elsie'll all get our work done and go to God. And so will Rosie. And we'll all see the dear Lord and the blessed Mother and all the angels and saints sitting round on their thrones, and all the flowers'll be out, like as it might be in my garden. And all the roses. And St. Peter'll let us in, and the dear Lord'll find our places for us. And He'll show the Major his place, and Mrs. Graeme her place, and me my place, and the places for Teresa and Lucy and Jamie and Elsie. And then He'll say: 'And now what about Rosie?' And Rosie'll say: 'I wants to be in the miggle.' And then the Lord'll say: 'Have you been a very, very good gurl? Have you done what Teresa told yer? Have you played the games the others wanted? Because only a VERY good little gurl can sit in the miggle.'"

"A very good little gurl," agreed Rosie, pensively. "An' I'll be a very good little gurl an' sit in the miggle."

"Ar," said Mr. Job. "But you give yer mind to the bein' good. Now what'll yer do to be good now?"

Rosie thought. Then her fingers found their way to a diminutive pocket in her dress, from which, after much wrestling and disarrangement of her attire, she produced a pink sweet. It had stuck to the pocket, and was still hairy. This, with a smile Helen of Troy might have envied, she handed to the Major.

"I give my thweet to him, and be a good lil gurl and sit in the miggle . . . in heaven," she said.

The Major gingerly took the sweet that was thrust upon him. He regarded it. It was Philippa who saved the situation.

"Major Fotheringay mustn't have sweets before his dinner," she said firmly. "He must keep it."

This Rosie appreciated. She knew that women existed to forbid other people to have sweets at odd moments. Besides, her part was over. She slid off Mr. Job's knee.

"Now I go and find T'resa and Luthy an' Jamie an' Elthie." She had begun to make this statement as she slipped off Mr. Job's knee. By the time she had finished it, she was as far down the lane as her fat legs would carry her.

Mr. Job rose from the hedge where he had been sitting. "Nobody understands children but the Lord," he said meditatively. "You mind what He did with a child? 'He took a lil child, an' set 'im *in the midst.*' In the miggle, as you might say," he added.

Them Upstairs

"The pain of purgatory is a fire of love, of impatient yet tranquil desire, this hunger for God. It is felt in full intensity when the spirit is free of the body. . . . The greatest pains the souls in Purgatory endure proceed from their being sensible of something in themselves displeasing to God."—St. Catherine of Genoa.

Them Upstairs

"**Y**OU MUST ALLOW that there is an element of humour about it," said Father Guardian to Father Bonaventure. They were watching the departure of the local Tertiaries after their November meeting.

"It wouldn't be either Divine or human if there weren't," replied the other. But he smiled involuntarily. Fond as he was of saying that there was always an element of delicious humour in the ways of Providence, he had to admit to himself that at Blackcombe the Tertiaries would have provoked the laughter of sheer joy from their Seraphic Father.

You see, there was the Novice-Master, Barnabas Job, with his bowed legs and snub nose and wide grey eyes. There was Sister Clare, otherwise Mrs. Alastair Graeme, in her tailored suit and silver fox stole and beautiful gloves. There was Brother Ruffino—otherwise Major Fotheringay—now at this moment walking down the road between Mrs. Graeme and Barnabas Job, turning his single eyeglass now on one and now on the other as he listened to them with stiff military courtesy. There was the newly professed Mrs. Kent, who was housekeeper to Major Fotheringay, now Sister Elizabeth and someone quite different from the downhearted woman who had taken the post a few months ago. And there were two novices, Esmond Dentoun (who was writing a book on the Franciscan influence on European culture) and Dick Tomkins (who was biting his nails).

"Abominable fog," said Esmond Dentoun, turning up the collar of his coat. "Well, I suppose we must do as Father Bonaventure suggests, and offer it—along with other trials and troubles—for the Holy Souls."

"S'pose so," said Dick. It WAS a beastly afternoon, and he had a long walk before him, for his father's farm was a good three miles from the church.

"Only seven months now to our profession, Brother. My word, I shall be glad to be professed. When I am writing about all these old Father-Generals and Saints of the Order, it always seems to me that they stare out of the old pictures at me very sniffily, as much as to say: 'And what might a Novice be doing writing about Us?'"

Dick smiled. He knew Mr. Dentoun—Brother Leo—was talking like this to cheer him up, because he had sensed Dick's depression.

"Can I give you a lift?" Brother Leo indicated the long touring car that was waiting for him outside.

Ordinarily Dick—Brother Anthony, I should say—would have jumped at the chance; but today he shook his head.

"No, thanks, sir. I'm . . . I expect I'll walk back with Mr. Job."

"Sensible fellow," said Esmond Dentoun. "Worth fifty lifts in a car. Well, cheerio. Anybody want a lift?" he added, raising his voice so that it carried to the others who were standing and talking at the bottom of the monastery road. "Come on, Mrs. Graeme. Get you back to your husband before he expects you. Come on, Major. Come on, Mrs. Kent. I can drop you at The Corner House. Sorry I can't go two ways at once, Job. But Dick's going to walk with you."

The Esmond Dentoun of a few months ago would have refused to pack his car full of miscellaneous persons, but the Esmond Dentoun of a few months ago was dead and buried and his grave was continually jumped on by his successor, Brother Leo.

That he never forgot his death and resurrection were due to Barnabas Job was evident in the way he took leave of the old cobbler, with more than a shade of respect in his manner.

And Barnabas Job evidently had an affection for his convert.

"It was legs Pruvidence give me, not wheels," he said. "Not but what I ain't made 'em more of the shape er wheels," he added, with the little chuckle with which he always appreciated one of his own jokes against himself. "Comin' along er me, Dick Tomkins?"

"Yes please, Mr. Job."

A keen glance at the boy told Barnabas Job that something was wrong. Here was a "job," evidently.

"Very good. Rackon kittle'll be near to the bile by the time we gits back. Come in and have a cup er-tea. This fog gits down yer throat something cruel. Mebbe we might as well stop at the baker's for a few pennorth er crumpets."

Hum. It must be something pretty far wrong if the prospect of tea and crumpets wouldn't cheer Dick.

Pansy came to meet them—flinging his elastic black body along the road, his long ears flying, and then cringing and wriggling round his master's feet until Barnabas Job nearly fell over him.

"There ain't nothin' to beat a spannel-dog to welcome yer home," he said contentedly. "Rackon the Lord'll have to think out something very good to beat spannels for welcomin' yer at the gates of 'Eaven."

Dick grunted.

"'Cording to Father Bonaventure," he said. "You get Purgatory. I don't call a nice stiff burning with fire much of a welcome for a tired Christian."

The sermon this afternoon had been about the Holy Souls, as befitted a November meeting.

Mr. Job stooped down, caught Pansy, and put him into Dick's arms. Pansy lavished all the devotion of a bright pink tongue on Dick's defenceless neck and ears.

"You give yer mind to Pansy," said Barnabas Job. "D'yer rackon as 'Im as thought of makin' Pansy'll have thoughts that's in'uman? You leave Pruvidance be and reckerlect yer iggernerance."

"But," said Dick. "The Church teaches it."

"Same as it teaches the myst'ry of the Blessed Trinity," said Mr. Job. "Fer us to believe, not fer us to understand. There's fire *and* fire. J'ever 'ear Mr. Dentoun say: 'Can't stop to talk. Got to get 'ome to work. Genius burns'? D'yer rackon as 'e's swallered a candle?"

"'Tisn't the same," said Dick, pushing open the gate with his knee, and letting the wriggling spaniel leap out of his arms and up the steep path to the cottage. "I know Mr. Dentoun's talking about a kind of spiritual burning, but his kind doesn't hurt. The Purgatory kind does hurt. The Church teaches that."

"That it does," said Mr. Job, making his rheumatic way up the path. "For why? Because the fire of Purgatory's the goodness of God, and ef you're full of self, the goodness of God's onbearable. Onbearable."

He produced a key and unlocked the cottage, and led the way into the kitchen, where the kettle on the hob was singing softly to itself.

"There, now! We forgot the crumpets. Well, we'll 'ave to make do with dripping toast."

The business of getting tea occupied them for ten minutes or so, but when they had drawn the table to the fire, and were sitting on either side of the hearth, Mr. Job entrusted the making of the toast to Dick, and occupied himself with pouring out the strong tea he loved.

"Now," he said, pushing a blue-rimmed cup towards Dick, "mebbe I can make yer understand this way. When I was a lil feller, I was a bad lil feller, and I was never so bad daytimes, as I was evenings. I have heard say as all children and animiles gets wild about sundown, and that it's natural-like for to tire 'em out so they'll sleep. Rackon that's likely enough, fer the Lord's allus sensible in the way 'E makes us. Well I mind it. Come six o'clock, I'd be as slippery as an eel and mischeevious as a monkey. And my poor mother with two on 'em smaller nor me. I'd be out er the 'ouse and down the street and up to all kinds of what I didn't ought. And

then, when I couldn't keep me eyes open, back I'd come, creepin'
into the back kitchen, wheedlin' round to me mother. And she'd
just look at me with them eyes of 'ers, and pick me up and carry me
upstairs, and lay me as I was in me bit of a bed. And I'd put up me
arms for a kiss, but she'd say: 'Mother can't kiss a dirty boy, and
she can't wash yer till yer sorry,' and then she'd go downstairs, and
leave me to think. And there I'd lie, and me 'eels'd be sore and the
skin off me knees and me mouth all sticky, too dirty ter be kissed.
I didn't want me wild ways then, but only a bit of motherin'. And
it 'ud seem a dreary long while—though I'd drop off to sleep off-
and-on, all oncomfertable—till I saw the light of 'er candle on the
passage wall, and I'd call out: 'Mammy, I'm sorry,' and along she'd
come, and a jug er warm water in 'er 'and, and wash the dirt off and
put something healing on me knees, and I'd drop off with me face
against 'er neck whiles she 'eld me in one arm and made me bed
with the other 'and.

"And I allus thinks of that," said Mr. Job, "along er Purgatory.
God sends us all to bed at the right time, and them as is obejent
gets washed afore they goes. And them as ain't, they lies there not
fit to be kissed until they've felt what it is to be dirty with disobe-
jence. And their knees burns where they've fallen down. 'Tain't
that they don't love their Mother—which is God. They came 'ome
right enough, but they loved their own way a good bit too. And so
there they lies, safe enough in their own beds, but not kissed yet.

"And," said Mr. Job, spreading dripping on the piece of toast
Dick passed him, "there's more to it. I 'ad a good brother. Willie, 'is
name was. Killed in the War 'e was, God reward 'im. Well, when
I'd been a bad lil feller, and I was up there all dirty and wantin' me
Mammy, time and again I'd 'ear Willie say: 'You leave the supper
things be, Mam. I'll wash 'em up. You get up to Alfie. Rackon 'e's
sorry now.' And that's very sim'lar to what we does when we prays
for the Pore Souls. 'I'll say these bits of prayers or do this good
work,' we sez, 'and You go and make them children of Yourn up

155

there comferble.' And that pleases 'Im, because every minute 'E's wantin' to get along and make them Pore Souls comferble, and you gives 'Im a kind er excuse to go a bit quicker. Now that's Purgatory as I sees it. And it's as bad for God as it is for them, as you might say, which is a mystery, God's bein' perfect 'n' therefore perfect in 'Is jy. But I remembers me mother's smile when she came to put me right, and I rackon I knows that it adds to the jy of God when 'E comes to make 'Eaven for the Pore Souls."

Dick stared at the crust of his toast.

"So praying for the dead gives God joy as well as . . . them?"

"Jy over one sinner doing penance," said Mr. Job. "'Eternal rest give them, O Lord. Go up and put 'em to rights, and I'll do this bit of a job in the back kitchen.' Sounds more sense than your way of thinkin', don't it? A Jew pedlar as I knew used ter say: 'God couldn't be everywhere, so 'E made mothers.' But them Jews always gets things a bit wrong, pore fellers. Fact is, God's everywhere all the time, and that's why 'E made mothers, to kinder give us a broad 'int. And ef it's bedtime for my immartel soul afore I've give over being self-willed-like, and I 'as to wait for me wash, I rackon I'll 'ear you or the Major say: 'You go along to Brother Barnabas as is upstairs, Lord; and I'll git on and do a job for You down 'ere.' And then 'E'll be that glad of the excuse, and come along quick, and I'll see 'Is Light coming along ter me, and I'll know I've got a good brother downstairs and . . .'"

"I see what you mean," said Dick with remarkable gruffness.

"You see," said Mr. Job, "when our dear Lord talked about 'fire' in 'Ell, rackon we kin take it 'E meant us to fear it as something terrible. And the Church ain't never said no more. That's all we know. But we know that the fire er purgatory's cleansin', same as earthly fire is. And we'll all be glad to put a lot er things we'm ashamed of on that rubbidge 'eap. It'll burn clean, same as eye-y-dine on a dirty wound. It'll burn up pride an' 'umbug. Wot we'm sorry for but wot still sticks to us. It's terrible *kind* fire, wotever it is. Wotever it is. I sez—but we knows wot it is. It's the good-ness of God—more cleansin', more warmin', more piercin' than fire, reachin' to the marrer of the soul. It won't terrify yer, but it's terrible, some'ow. It'll send yer all grievin' and lovin' and achin' that yer weren't better. God allus does things gentle. Mind that. I knows that's right, for I 'ad it from Father Guardian. Bein' put in yer bed dirty is very gentle, but the look in the Lord's Eyes'll be piercin' tender and yer'll want to be kissed terrible bad. Would yer like to say the rosary for Them Upstairs after tea?"

"All right. I don't mind," said Dick with ill-disguised willing-ness. He turned in his chair and sought to change the subject be-cause the problem had been solved and his heart was full. "Fog's lifted."

"Rackon it 'as," said Barnabas Job drily. "God don't make fogs. Them's jest 'uman iggernerance. But 'E's got a fine lot er stars be'ind."

A Real Christmas

"Only where He was homeless
Are you and I at home."

G. K. CHESTERTON.

A Real Christmas

SNOW LAY in deep drifts over Mr. Job's garden, and across the fields and down the roads and through the woods as far as the eye could see there was evidence that it was real Christmas weather. The stars trembled in the arch of sky, dark and blue as the mantle of the Madonna. All was silence, but here and there in the village and in the far distance a window shone bright or rosy, and you knew that a lamp had been left burning for those who had gone to Midnight Mass, or else that some children could not sleep for excitement about "stockings," or busy mothers were late in playing cook or Santa Claus.

The silence was broken by a noise that did not seem to fit into it—not a bell, or the bark of a dog, or a voice; but the sudden twang of a gate, a stealthy, nervous noise. And a dark figure crept up Mr. Job's steep path, leaving small footmarks black in the snow. (He himself had gone to Mass out of the back gate, and the front path was virginally white.) Whoever it was, the late comer had no right there, that was certain from the way of his—or her—arrival. The queer thing was, the figure seemed to melt into the darkness of the porch, and stay there, motionless. Queer. Very odd indeed. And nothing but the arrival of Barnabas Job would solve the problem of the burglar, ghost or . . . or what?

The arrival of Barnabas Job was characteristic. He came with Pansy at his heels, his missal under his arm, and a dim tune on his lips, a faint old melody of some forgotten carol. He shut his gate carefully, lifting the latch with the deliberateness of a man who has not always had a gate of his own to shut, and who has not lost the joy of his possession. Then he plodded up the path. But suddenly he stopped short to get his breath, and realised the meaning of the footsteps. Village folk didn't come calling at that hour. Small stout shoes. He looked ahead at the porch, but could discern nothing, until he drew near . . . and by then Pansy had dashed ahead, and Mr. Job heard a gasp.

"Alright," he said. "Alright. Pansy won't 'urt you. Pansy, come 'ere."

He took another step forward, and peering into the darkness of the porch, saw a woman sitting there, wrapped in an old black coat much too large for her. She just sat there, looking at him, so he pulled off his hat.

"Can I do anythink fer you, ma'am?" he asked, with that courtesy which he had not learnt in any school of manners in this world.

"Alf," she said, with a sob, and stretched out a pair of the thinnest hands a woman could have.

It was many years since anyone had called Barnabas Job by his unregenerate name.

"What's this?" he said. "Are you somebody I did ought to reckerlect?"

"Alf . . . it's Becky."

For a moment his heart stood still, and then he had taken a big step forward, and covered those thin hands with his own horny brown ones.

"You've been a main long time comin', my gurl," he said.

"I didn't have nowhere else," she said with the truthfulness of those who are too hopeless even to try and make the best of a last chance.

"Well, yer don't need two places," said Mr. Job. "Leastways, not unless ye're a Countess," he added with an attempt to joke away the emotion of the moment. "'Arf a mo' while I strike a light."

He was so quick in the way he moved about, she noted dully. In a flash he had lit the lamp and put a match to the fire (which he had raked out and laid fresh for the morning—no matter). And then he brought her in, and shut the door, and led her to the old wicker armchair with its faded cretonne cushions.

"Set down and get a warm," he said. "No good startin' to talk until kittle's bilin'. Rackon mebbe you bin waitin' some time."

"Good long time," she replied, but cared little for that or anything, it was evident.

Dazed with cold, weariness and hopelessness, she watched him prepare a meal that she thought of as a very late supper, but which to him was a very early breakfast. From larder to kitchen he ran like a boy, fetching bread and butter and bacon and eggs. He brandished a frying-pan. He broke the eggs. He slapped in the bacon deftly. He put a toasting-fork in Becky's hand, and she found herself mechanically making the bread steam and brown before the red glow between the bars of the kitchen grate.

And so, before very long, with the contents of the frying-pan on their plates, and the brown teapot in its red and green hairpin-work cover between them, they were sitting down to their meal at half-past two a.m. on Christmas morning. It was only when Pansy had licked the plates, and Becky had shaken her head at the honey jar, that Barnabas pulled out his pipe, asked Becky's permission, and stuffing in tobacco asked:

"Well, my dear?"

"Well," she said. "Reckon you thought I'd come one day."

"Ar."

"Well, I've come."

"Thank God fer that."

"Ar. You wait a bit with yer 'Thank God's.' I din 'ave no wheres else. 'E bin and left me. After fifteen years and all I stuck by 'im through. Well, let 'im go. But reckon you're pleased it's come as you said—and me with no claim on 'im, not 'avin' me lines."

Mr. Job looked at her, and saw not the worn face of the woman for whom he had prayed during those fifteen years in which she had given up the practice of her religion for a worthless man who had never married her, but the little sister whom he had protected from their drunken father forty years ago.

"Rackon I'm pleased you've come," he said, his broad country speech sounding homely in comparison with hers. "That's all there is to it. I never let my back room here, and it's bin ready fer you all along. Sun got in, along er my keepin' it aired, and spiled the paper; so I did it up last Easter. Sevenpence the piece, I paid. Very tasty pattern er blue roses. And a nice pink quilt."

Then he hesitated, remembering something.

"But . . . fact is, my dear . . . I'm afraid. . . ."

"I can get gorn," she said, moving—guessing the worst from habit in the way that the saddest of human creatures are wont to do.

"Set still. You bide here. You did ought to 'a bin 'ere all the time. But it's about our dinner termorrer. That's my lack er faith. Pray, pray all the time fer our Becky to come 'ome, and never take no precautions. Me and Pansy are one thing, but rackon it's plum lack er faith not to keep a tin er somethink extra in case."

Because she looked bewildered, he grinned at his own complex thought.

"It's like this," he said, like a boy who has been caught up an apple tree. "It's a fancy of mine to 'ave a pertickler *real* kind of Christmas, same as the Lord. 'E didn' 'ave plum-puddin' and turkey. Wot did 'E 'ave? Milk and the cold and only the beasts to warm 'Im. So me and Pansy, we likes it like that. 'E 'as a bit of sossidge, along of being only a pup, but milk not agreein' with me pertickler, I jest takes a bit of bread and cheese and a cup er-tea, and we 'as our Christmas dinner in the barn yonder, along of the cows. And so, yer see, I ain't got much in the larder, and shops is shut, and termorrer's Boxing Day and the day after that's Sunday . . ."

Rebecca Jenkins looked at him with her stern grey eyes, no less stern now in their setting of tired wrinkles than when they had glared at the father she hated. They were eyes that had never learnt to look gentle.

"What suits you'll suit me," she said. "Anyways, it's better than nothink by a long chalk. But don't you fergit this, Alfie. I ain't got no faith. You can't 'ave everythink taken from you and keep yer faith."

"Can't yer?" said Barnabas. "Now that's jest where I don't agree with yer. Didn' I lose everythink when I lost my Jessie? D'yer rackon I wanted the world after she'd done with it? Wasn't it all taken from me, and worse than taken from me when she went? I couldn't look at a buttercup, nor walk round the roads, but they all minded me of 'er, and she dead. And ain't it all still taken? This ain't mine, this cottage. 'Tis God's cottage as I'm a usin' fer 'Im. Kind of a caretaker. That's God's kittle, and that's God's teapot, and Pansy's God's lil spannel-dog,—when 'e ain't the divil's along of 'is bein' only 'arf convarted. And me 'ands and me mind—they ain't mine. Rackon I'd any use for them when she'd gone, and I'd never touch 'er no more, and never think out things to please 'er no more? She's a saint, and I ain't near 'er, unless I'm doing me best. But when I'm servin' the Lord, then she and me's workin' together."

His voice was trembling and his hands were shaking as he broke the silence of years.

"You ain't a saint if yer keeps anythink fer yerself. You can't keep anythink fer yerself in 'Eaven. It all turns to God's purpose like a sunflower to the sun. So ef I keeps anythink fer meself, rackon it's between me and Jessie. So I use it fer the Lord or else give it away. I don't keep nothin' but 'Im and Jessie. And I can't give away Jessie, because 'E's keepin' 'er fer me."

"Ain't God enough fer you, then?" she asked, with the petty malice of the sore in heart.

"Ar," he replied tranquilly. "'E's enough fer 'Imself, but 'E was minded to make me to love 'Im; and 'E's enough fer me, but 'E was minded to make my Jessie to love me and me to love Jessie so we'd 'ave the more to thank 'Im for. God don't keep yer on iron rations—it's allus a feast when 'E 'as the spreadin' of it. And now 'E's bin and give me Becky fer a Christmas present."

With unconscious wisdom, he knew how overwrought she was with this desperate home-coming, driven in by the wolves of hunger and misery. The morning would be time enough for talk. And so he bid her go to bed.

He had fetched down the bedding when they first arrived and spread it before the fire, and a brick had been getting hot in readiness for encasing in a flannel bag and doing duty as a bed-warmer. Now they went upstairs, Barnabas leading the way with the feather bed, and Becky following with the pillow and covers. They made up the bed, and Barnabas wished her good night as casually as though he had done so every night for the past years. Then, shivering—for it did not occur to either of them that a fire could be lit in the tiny grate—Becky undressed. Before she lay down, she held up her candle and had a long look round the little room with its wall-paper decked with those fat blue roses and the washstand and chest of drawers painted yellow and grained to imitate some unheard-of wood. There was a picture of the Sacred Heart like a conflagration over the mantelpiece, but to Rebecca Jenkins it was a guest-chamber in one of the many mansions of Heaven. Then she blew out the candle, lay down, and would have cried herself to sleep, only she was too weary.

No other Mass that morning for Barnabas. He could not go out and leave Becky, nor was she fit to walk down the long road to church and face curious villagers.

She came down about nine, and found him already whistling about the scullery, washing up the remains of the midnight meal. Unobtrusively she began to find where things were kept, and to lay the breakfast. The heart of Barnabas sang within him, but he made no comment.

When dinner-time came, she insisted on carrying the bread and cheese and the jug of cocoa across into the neighbouring barn, and would not hear of Barnabas making any alteration in his customs for her. After the meal, Pansy climbed into her lap, and she sat there in the hay with the stillness of a spent swimmer attaining the shore. Emotionally she was exhausted. She asked nothing better than to sit still, listening to the gentle movements of the cows in the byre, of hoof on cobblestones or creaking manger. Barnabas sat by the tiny window, wrapped as she was in an old coat, knee-deep in the hay, reading his Bible and saying his rosary and often pausing to listen to the cows in a kind of ecstasy.

It was not until the early twilight of the winter afternoon darkened the barn that he rose and went down, pushing his way carefully between Bossy and Buttercup, laying his kind old hand on their warm flanks, and stooping to kiss the manger. Then he came round and held out his hand to Becky.

"Rackon we've rested alongside Our Blessed Lady and St. Joseph," he said. "And now we did ought to got back fer to get you some tea, my dear. Seein' you there, sims to me the little Lord's give 'Isself a Christmas present. Rackon this 'as bin a real Christmas."

Our Mam

"She seems to reproduce on earth the Divine, the simple Being. She is so transparent that we might mistake her for the Light itself, yet she is only the Mirror of the Sun of Justice. It seems to me that she is more easy to imitate than any other saint: it brings me peace whenever I look at her."—SISTER ELIZABETH OF THE TRINITY.

Our Mam

HE LAST DAY of the year dawned bright. A Christmas rose and some yellow stars of aconite were in bloom in a sheltered corner of the garden. Indeed, it seemed to Barnabas that the whole of his home rejoiced in the accession of Becky—the stocky little woman with the deep-set eyes—to the throne, or rather the windsor armchair, at the head of the table. What cottage could do less, when Becky scrubbed and polished from morning to night, washed and ironed (with scorn for Barnabas's simple attempts at laundry)?

This morning, she had searched in vain for her blue bag, only to find, when at last she asked Barnabas if he had seen it, that he was using it himself, out there in the garden, ground into a saucerful of turpentine, wherewith to colour Our Lady's statue.

"And not a pinch left," she scolded unfrowning, feeling the winter sunshine warm on her bare arms, though the wind blew bitterly cold now and then. "How d'you reckon I'm a-goin' to get up yer shirt for tomorrow?"

"Wash it and iron it, my dear," he said tranquilly, taking the pipe out of his mouth to answer. "It'll do for once without bluein'."

"For once! By the look of it, you uses all yer blue bags the same way! It's yeller as butter." She stood watching his nimble old fingers at work, sweeping the brush down the folds of Our Lady's mantle. "What d'you call this one? Our Lady of Good Counsel, or what?"

"Seat of Wisdom," he said, the brush following tenderly the long lines of the graceful figure whose crowned head bent

171

towards the Child asleep on her shoulder, clasping his little cross with one baby hand.

"Wonder what made 'em think of callin' it that?" Becky mused, her mind half on the statue and half on the thin places in Barnabas' best shirt. "Where did you get it?"

"Father Boneyvencher give it me," replied Barnabas. "Come out er some church. Somebody give 'em a grander one. Truth was, the Lord meant it fer me. Don't it mind you of our Mam puttin' me to bed after I'd bin washed and forgiven?"

Becky was rather shocked. (The one-time sinner is generally more easily shocked than the innocent of heart when it comes to a certain homeliness with holy things. That is one of the penalties. The wounds of sins may be healed—Becky had been to confession the previous day for the first time for fifteen years—but they are wont to leave a certain stiffness, which makes it difficult for the soul to *play in His sight*. It is hard to forgo the preoccupation with self-hatred, and to enter into the joy of the angels as generously as God forgives. It is common enough for a sinner to be shocked at God's offer to forget what He has forgiven, and to think wiser to send oneself to Coventry for a while or to behave with constraint towards the rejoicing angels.)

"'E din need to be washed and forgiven," she said primly.

"That ain't 'Im," said Barnabas serenely, caressing the statue with his brush. "That's me."

"I don't call that kind of 'magination very respectful," said Becky.

"Oo does?" demanded Barnabas, stopping, brush in air, so that the blue ran down his finger. "Oo wants to? And oo calls it 'magination? Lack er faith, that's wot it is. What did 'E say: 'Son, be'old thy Mother.'. . . My lawks," he continued, as the wind blew piercingly against his brown cheek, and the sun went in, "rackon I can't 'old this brush fer the cold. Mind if I brings the job inter the back kitchen?"

"Please yerself," said Becky amicably. "So long as you keeps that turps out er my copper."

She led the way, taking the saucer of Reckitt's, while Barnabas gingerly carried the heavy half-painted statue into the warm back kitchen where the fire was alight under the copper.

He set down his burden and straightened his back. Then he waved his hand towards his old cobbler's bench which had been pushed to one side.

"You 'ave a set down while yer washing biles," he said to Becky. "You gotter listen to me, my dear. You got it all wrong about the Blessed Mother."

Becky found obedience to Barnabas very restful, and did as she was bidden.

"Now," said her brother, dipping his brush in the colour and getting to work again, "you learn this from Our Lady Seat of Wisdom: 'tain't respect we oughter show—as she might be Squire's lady— 'tis somethin' much sweeter, my dear. What 'E said, if you reckerlect, was: 'Except you becomes as little children, you can't enter the Kingdom er Heaven.' Little children ain't respectful—not natural, they ain't—they'm jest . . . wonderin' and . . . biddable and, *askin'*." He had ruffled his grey hair with the end of the paint-brush in seeking the right word, and there was a trickle of paint down his wrist of which he was supremely unaware. "That's where so many makes a mistake," he went on. "They keeps being respectful and keepin' their place when the Lord wants them to run right into 'Is Sacred 'Eart. And yet," he said, shaking his head, "the Lord couldn't ha' spoke plainer. 'E did 'Is best to get us to fergit about bein' respectful and to see as 'E meant us to begin by bein' children."

He stood there, the bow-legged, lean old man in his darned grey cardigan with the scarlet and purple neckerchief, painting away.

"You rackon it all up," he said. "'Ave you ever thought wot God A'mighty wanted Mary for at all? Why didn' 'E jest send 'Is Son down as a little Baby fer them shepherds to find there in the snow with the angels singin' round? Rackon that 'ud 'ave been as good, and mebbe the shepherds 'ud 'ave thought a deal of a Baby as the angels sang round. But, only thing is—'E didn't. 'They found the young Child with Mary 'Is Mother.' Ar. And what for did God A'mighty want fer to leave 'Im with 'er fer thirty years and give 'Is apostles only three? What for did 'E want to make 'Im do 'Is first merrickle when she asked, even though 'E said 'Is time wasn't come? Could 'E say plainer that if we was born again to eternal life we got to 'ave a mother, and we got to stay with 'er and mind what she says? Rackon we knows better than God A'mighty and can manage without 'er, we do. Ar. Onnatural. And you mark wot comes of it," he went on, pointing his brush at her and dropping a spot of celestial colour on the flagstones. "Didn' all the Apostles fersake 'Im and flee? Yes, they did. 'Scept oo? 'Scept St. John and Mary Magdalen. Fer why? Rackon it was along of them stayin' beside 'Is Mother. 'Twer the safest place, same as 'tis now if you don't want to do anything to 'urt 'Im. She knows wot 'E wants."

He stood back and surveyed the statue, now almost finished.

"And wot were the very last thing 'E give away, like? 'Son, be'old thy Mother. Mother, be'old thy son. And the disciple took 'er fer 'is own.' Which is jest wot 'E wants us to do, only we'm that slow in the uptake."

He tore a piece of newspaper off that on which the statue was standing, placed over the table by the careful Becky, and wiped his brush.

"And that's wot I done," he said reminiscently. "Took 'er for me own. When Father Boneyvencher done explaining and left me alone with 'er in this cottage, I sez: 'Our Mam,' I sez, 'you knows 'Is ways, and you knows 'em better than the Apostles theirselves, and you put it into me 'eart to do wot 'E'd fancy. Alfred Jenkins is dead,' I sez, 'Drowned in baptism, as it were,' I sez, 'And this yere is your son, Barnabas Job, and rackon 'e'd better begin by bein' subjeck to yer fer to grow in grace, same as Jesus Christ wot was God and didn't disdain so to do. And it was queer," he said, a smile playing round his wide mouth, "me as was fifty and 'ad seen a bit er loife, I got to fergit everything 'scept askin' 'er wot 'E wanted done. And I'd think a bit, and ask 'er, and it 'ud come into my mind quiet and warm as that sunshine—jest like a bit of quiet where there'd bin a noise—and I'd know. Seemed as I fergot all I'd learnt, and she were all my wisdom. And it's a queer thing," he said, helping himself out of the pot which contained the brick-dust for "redding-up" the front step, and preparing to attend to the complexion of the statue, "Never once does she talk about 'erself. Never 'I wants this done.' D'yer mind our Mam, Becky? 'Yer father sez . . .' 'Yer father wants . . .' Well, she allus made out as 'e was a good father till she couldn't no longer, and that killed 'er. But when *she*," he indicated the statue, "sez: 'Yer Father who art in 'Eaven,' she don't 'ave to pretend. She knows 'E's infinitely good. Many a time I've said to 'er: 'Our Mam, when's my Becky comin' back?' And she'd say: 'Yer Father sez: Ask, and you shall receive.'"

"Oh dear," said Becky. "Well, it were a bit too late. Reckon it's all right fer you, Alfie. But if I got callin' 'er 'Our Mam' I'd expect a thunderbolt to strike me dumb."

"That's iggernerance," said Barnabas serenely. "And to be excused because you 'aven't read the 'oly Gospel fer many a long day. You weren't one of them plain painted bad lots, and you never 'ad seven devils cast out er you. Yet a plain painted bad lot Mary Magdalen was and seven devils was cast out'n of 'er—and yet she stayed with Our Lord's Mother. 'Er eldest darter, as you might say. Ar. Mary Magdalen gave 'Im spices in an alambaster box, and 'E gave 'er the sweetest thing 'E got—the Tower er Ivory where 'E'd dwelt. You give your best to 'Im and 'E'll give 'Is best to you. And if you notice, arter Mary Magdalen'd bin with Our Blessed Lady, sims as though Our Lady let 'er begin all over new—as though 'er sin worn't not only fergiven, but as though God A'mighty and 'Oly Church clean fergot it. You mind the Litanies. Didn' the Church put 'er first among the virgins?"

Becky stared. She would have denied it if she could, with the top-heavy self-hatred that was hers. It seemed to her too good—preposterously and wrongly too good—for any sinner.

"It don't seem right," she said. "Leastways . . . maybe for St. Magdalen . . ."

Barnabas thumped his knee.

"What business is it of your'n?" he demanded. "Is it fer you, Becky Jenkins, to say what God A'mighty shall or shan't do?"

"I never meant that," she said hastily.

"More you don't. Nobody don't. But a powerful deal er folks talks like it, and they *thinks* like it. Full er their own sense, they are. Full er self, even when they'm sorry. Ar. Our Lady ain't like that. She'm so empty 'erself that God could do wot 'E liked with 'er. Like a lil clear pool wot reflects the sun. That's wot she does. Reflects 'Is Goodness. ''E 'as filled the 'ungry with good things!' And always on about wot a pity it is to be rich and mighty because the likes of them ain't got room for nothin' but theirselves. They can't get nothin' but the grace to be took down and sent away 'ungry to think it over. Then yer see, when they *are* 'ungry, 'E fills 'em with good things."

He stood back to look at the statue which smiled with pale brick-dusted lips.

"That's wot she've larned me," he said. "Seat of Wisdom. Larns you as you don't know nothing."

Becky had come close to inspect her brother's handiwork.

"Why's 'E got that cross?" she asked, pointing to the Child.

"That's 'Is lesson-book," said Barnabas.

"What," said Becky, "learn a baby like that all about sufferin'?"

"'E began larnin' out er that lesson-book soon as 'E was born," said Barnabas. "But 'E 'ad 'Is Mother. But I tells you, mebbe that's 'Im, but in a manner of speakin' it's me too, and you, and St. John, and St. Magdalen, and all of us. And that's all we did ought er 'ave—our little crawss and our Mam."

Even the spaniel, who had gone to sleep under the table, seemed to have put himself under the protection of her in whom God became incarnate by the overshadowing of the Third Person of the Blessed Trinity. The graceful figure of the woman, royal of birth and village bred, whose obedience to the Angel's message repaired the disobedience of Eve tempted by the Fallen Angel: Mary, Mother of Him who had God for His Father, simplest, purest of creatures, at whose knee and against whose heart the children of the Second Adam were to learn again lost wisdom, and find lost innocence . . . to consider her is to lay aside our preconceived notions, and become docile to the Will of God.

"Seat of Wisdom," said Barnabas. "She'll learn you the secrets of the 'Eart of God. And she'll teach you to play, same as children did ought to. And she'll let you do odd jobs. You ask 'er to give you somethink to do all day long for 'Im, and rackon you'll discover very slow and sure wot 'E meant you for when 'E made you."

"At this time of day?" said Becky, slow of heart.

"Rackon you fergits," said Barnabas with his crooked smile. "God only give you to 'er Christmas night. You'm the littlest one."

ALSO BY CECILY HALLACK

View a sample chapter from each title at www.staidanpress.com.

THE HAPPINESS OF FATHER HAPPÉ

Shingle Bay did not know what to make of Fr. Savinius Happé. He was a cheerful, rotund Franciscan, a famous author of books on everything from Etruscan civilization to Alpine meadows to beetles, and someone who had never quite mastered the English language. His jovial demeanor concealed a wisdom that alternately bewildered, astonished, but ultimately won over the people of Shingle Bay.

$10.00 — 112 pages. Available at amazon.com.

OTHER TITLES AVAILABLE FROM ST. AIDAN PRESS

THE QUEEN'S TRAGEDY
by Msgr. Robert Hugh Benson

"Upon the publication of former books of mine several kindly critics remarked that the reign of Mary Tudor told a very different story with regard to the Catholic character. It is that story which I am now attempting to set forth as honestly as I can."

$19.00 — 364 pages. Available at amazon.com.

THE NET
by Agnes Blundell

"Roger felt a freezing dew break out upon his forehead. The net was over him it seemed; in vain he told himself that he could establish his identity. His head was worth forty pounds to the vile creatures at the stair foot, and once in their clutches who knew if he could ever communicate with his friends? . . . Gaolers and pursuivants alike fattened on the traffic in human life and divided the spoils. Judges were as careless as callous."

$16.00 — 264 pages. Available at amazon.com.

THE ANCHORHOLD
by Enid Dinnis

Editha de Beauville had all that the world could offer: wealth, wit, and beauty. Yet a chaplain's sermon drove her to give up all this, and enter the religious life. But could a proud, strong-willed noblewoman accept and embrace the poverty and self-abnegation of the religious life, particularly that of full seclusion in an anchorhold? A difficult path lay before Editha. Read on to learn how she fared, and how her life affected those around her, including Sir Aleric, her erstwhile suitor, now a crusader knight; Fr. Nicholas, a young priest who was quite bright, and thought so too; and Fiddlemee, the witty yet wise court jester whose past held a surprising secret.

$14.00 — 194 pages. Available at amazon.com.

THE SHEPHERD OF WEEPINGWOLD
by Enid Dinnis

Sir Robert Luffkyn, rich grandson of a peasant, has purchased the manor of Weepingwold from the noble but impoverished de Lessels, intending to make the renamed Luffkynwold a busy center of his tanning trade. He sends Petronilla, last de Lessels, to Gracerood, intending her for its future Abbess, and plucks little Brother Kit from the cloister to become the new parson of the long-abandoned church. How will Father Kit fare with the parish and his own soul? Will Petronilla find her true vocation? And is there really a witch in the parish?

$14.00 — 202 pages. Available at amazon.com.

SCOUTING FOR SECRET SERVICE
by Fr. Bernard F. J. Dooley

Frank and George are going to spend their summer vacation in the Adirondacks, thanks to Frank's uncle Ed. But once they get there, they realize something fishy is going on. Can they trust Pete, their Indian guide, or is he mixed up in it too? And is Frank's mysterious uncle really behind it all?

$14.00 — 188 pages. Available at amazon.com.

CON OF MISTY MOUNTAIN
by Mary T. Waggaman

"It had been a long night for Con. Just what had happened to him he was at first too dazed to know. Dennis had flung him into the smoking-room with no very gentle hand, turned the key and left him to himself. And, sinking down dully upon a rug that felt very soft and warm after the hard flight over the mountain, Con was glad to rest his bruised, aching limbs, his dizzy head, without any thought of what was to come upon him next."

$14.00 — 190 pages. Available at amazon.com.

NON-FICTION

CATHOLICISM AND SCOTLAND
by Compton Mackenzie

Much has been written about the desperate fight that English Catholics waged to keep the Faith, but Scotland's Catholic history is little known. Have you ever heard of David Beaton, Cardinal Archbishop of St. Andrews, and his struggles? Or of Fr. Ninian Winzet, who boldly challenged Calvinist champion John Knox to a public debate? Read this book and find out about the Scots who sought to defend their country and their Faith from the onslaught of Protestantism.

$12.00 — 138 pages. Available at amazon.com.

www.ingramcontent.com/pod-product-compliance
Lightning Source LLC
Chambersburg PA
CBHW020752210626
46807CB00018B/2663